"Annie, I [...] I want to ask [...]"

She looked up, surprised by Alex's serious tone. "Sure. What is it?"

"My grandmother needs someone to live with her when she comes home, until she recovers."

She thought about that for a moment, then slowly shook her head. "I'm sorry, Alex. I'd love to stay with Irene, but I have a business to run and a daughter to support."

His eyebrows rose. "A daughter?"

Her stomach clenched. She'd thought he knew about Emma. But how would he? She was just a former employee who got on the wrong track and found herself in a whole lot of trouble.

Slipping her hands into her jacket pockets, she pushed those painful thoughts away. It didn't matter now. She'd made her choices and she had to live with them.

She looked up and met his curious gaze. "Yes, I have a five-year-old daughter, Emma."

There was so much more to the story, but she wasn't sure if he wanted to hear it—or if she had the courage to tell him.

Books by Carrie Turansky

Love Inspired

Along Came Love
Seeking His Love
A Man to Trust
Snowflake Sweethearts

CARRIE TURANSKY

is an award-winning author of ten novels and novellas. She has been a finalist for an Inspirational Readers' Choice Award and an ACFW Genesis Award and winner of an ACFW Carol Award and Crystal Globe Award. Carrie writes contemporary and historical romance for Barbour Publishing and Love Inspired Books. She lives in central New Jersey with her husband, Scott, who is a pastor, author, speaker and counselor. They have five young adult children and three grandchildren. Carrie leads women's ministry at her church, and when she is not writing she enjoys gardening, reading, flower arranging and cooking for friends and family. Her website is www.carrieturansky.com.

Snowflake Sweethearts

Carrie Turansky

Love Inspired

™ LOVE INSPIRED BOOKS

ISBN-13: 978-0-373-87785-0

SNOWFLAKE SWEETHEARTS

www.LoveInspiredBooks.com

Printed in U.S.A.

Bear with each other and forgive whatever
grievances you may have against one another.
Forgive as the Lord forgave you. And over all
these virtues put on love, which
binds them all together in perfect unity.

—*Colossians* 3:13, 14

To Grace, Jenn, Terry and Judy,
who encourage me with their caring friendship.
May the love you give be multiplied back to you!

Chapter One

Annie Romano tucked the loose end of her red wool scarf into the front of her jacket and snuggled down into the soft lining. Puffing out a breath, she tried to warm her chilly face as she waited at the corner of Eleventh and Harris in the historic district of Fairhaven, Washington. A brisk, early-November breeze blew up the hill, carrying the fresh, salty scent of Bellingham Bay.

Clenching her hands in her pockets, she gazed across the street at Jameson's Bakery and lifted a silent prayer. *Please, God, help me find a job. Not just for my sake, but also for Emma's.*

With her stomach knotting in a tight ball, she stepped off the curb and crossed the street. It wasn't that she didn't want to see Irene Jameson, or that she was afraid to ask her for a job. The sweet, elderly owner of Jameson's Bakery had always treated her kindly. But seven years had passed since Annie left Fairhaven, and her life had taken some drastic turns since then.

What would Irene say about Annie's daughter, Emma?

A powerful mixture of love and guilt rose and battled in her heart, but love won. She pressed the guilt deeper away to deal with another time.

Straightening her shoulders, she pushed open the front door. A bell jingled overhead. The delicious scent of cinnamon and freshly baked bread filled the air. Her mouth watered, and sweet memories came flooding back.

It wasn't just Irene's kindness or the tempting bakery treats that had kept her working at Jameson's when she was a teenager. She'd had a huge crush on Irene's grandson, Alex, who also worked there. But Alex had left for college when she was only fifteen, long before she had the courage to tell him how she felt.

Regret burned her throat. She wished now that she'd made more of an effort to stay in touch with Alex and Irene. But when she'd left Fairhaven after high school, she hadn't thought she would ever come back.

Muted conversation drifted from the bakery kitchen. "Be right there," Irene called, then stepped through the doorway wearing her familiar smile. "Good morning." Her eyes widened and she gasped. "Annie? Is that really you?"

Annie smiled and nodded. "Hi, Irene."

The plump owner of Jameson's walked with a halting sway as she came around the end of the bakery case and enveloped Annie in a warm, fleshy hug. "Oh, it's so wonderful to see you."

"Good to see you, too."

Irene stepped back. "My goodness, just look at you. You're lovely."

Annie blushed and shook her head. Contacts had replaced her glasses, and her smile was free of braces, but she'd never classify herself as lovely.

"Oh, I'm so glad you didn't cut off all those gorgeous curls." Irene reached out and touched a strand of Annie's hair.

"I threaten to at least once a week."

"Well, don't you dare!" Irene motioned toward one of the four small tables lined up by the front windows. "Can I get you a cup of coffee? How about an apple fritter? I remember those were always your favorite."

"No, thanks." Annie didn't have any money to spare, though the thought of those melt-in-your-mouth treats made her empty stomach quiver.

Irene tipped her head, and her double chin sagged to the left. "Are you sure, honey?" She pulled a paper napkin from her apron pocket and swiped at her glistening nose and cheeks. "We've got some fresh pumpkin muffins or blueberry cake doughnuts if you'd rather have one of those." Her hand shook slightly as she tucked the napkin away.

"No. I'm okay." But Annie wondered if the same was true of her friend. She looked heavier and had aged quite a bit since she'd seen her last.

"Let's sit down." Irene pulled out a chair and lowered herself into it with a heavy sigh. "My poor old knees are complaining today." She smiled across the table, but it didn't erase the weary lines around her eyes and mouth. "How have you been, Annie? It's been ages since I've seen you. Are you back in town to visit friends?"

"Actually, I moved back to Fairhaven a couple months ago. I wanted to get settled in time for my daughter, Emma, to start kindergarten."

Irene's eyebrows rose, but her smile didn't falter. "Oh, that's wonderful. I didn't realize she was already five. Do you have a picture of her?"

Annie's heart lifted. She should've known Irene would be as warm and caring as she'd always been. She took a photo of Emma from her purse and handed it to Irene. "That was taken at our church's Fourth of July picnic in Portland, before we moved up here."

"Oh, she's beautiful. She looks just like you with those big brown eyes and dark curls."

"Thanks." Annie tucked the photo back in her purse. "I

want Emma to grow up here in Fairhaven, where it's safe and she'll get a good education."

"Of course you do. I'm sure you're a wonderful mother."

Annie shifted in her chair. She needed to get to the point of her visit. "I worked my way through culinary school in Portland, and I've started my own business here in Fairhaven as a personal chef."

"Oh, that's great. You always were creative in the kitchen. How's it going?"

"I have a few clients, but not enough to support us. I need to find a part-time job." She hesitated, hoping Irene would understand where she was going, but the older lady simply nodded and waited for her to continue.

"So…I was wondering if you need any help here at the bakery."

Irene's smile faltered. "Oh, honey, I'd love to hire you again." She glanced toward the kitchen and lowered her voice. "But the truth is, business has been pretty slow. I'm barely able to pay Harry, and I had to cut back on Janelle's and Clyde's hours. I'm sorry."

Annie's hopes deflated, but she forced a small smile. "It's all right. I'm sure I'll find something."

"Of course you will. You're a good worker. I'd hire you in a minute if I could." Her smile returned. "Say, why don't you put me down as a reference? I'll give a glowing report to anyone who calls."

Annie forced a smile. "Thanks, I'd appreciate that." But she had few other connections in Fairhaven and no idea who else might hire her.

Irene patted her hand with cool, clammy fingers. "Now, don't worry. Just pray and trust the Lord, and something will work out. You'll see." She glanced toward the kitchen again. "Why don't I tell Harry you're here? I'm sure he'll want to come out and say hello." She rose and stepped away from the table, then swayed slightly. Her hands shot out as if she was trying to regain her balance.

Annie's heart lurched. "Irene, are you all right?"

Irene lifted a trembling hand to her forehead. "I'm sure I'll be fine…in a minute." But her face had gone pasty pale, and her eyes fluttered as she searched the room.

Annie jumped up and reached for her friend. "Irene, what is it? What's wrong?"

"Oh…Annie." Irene grimaced and clutched her apron over her chest. Her eyes widened and anguish flashed across her face, then she crumpled.

"Irene!" Annie lunged to catch her before she hit the floor. Adrenaline shot through her as she grasped Irene's shoulders and lifted her head. "Harry! Harry, come quick!"

"What's going on?" The old baker hustled through the kitchen doorway, spotted Annie and Irene on the floor, and gasped.

"Call 9-1-1! Hurry!" Annie's stomach roiled as she searched Irene's pale face. *Oh, God, please have mercy.*

Alex Jameson strode through the main entrance of St. Joseph's Medical Center and headed for the front desk. "Can you tell me the room number for Irene Jameson?"

The elderly woman behind the desk pushed her silver-rimmed glasses up her nose then slowly tapped the computer keys. A few seconds passed before she finally looked up. "She's not listed."

A huge fist lodged in his throat. Was he too late? No, he couldn't be. "I'm sure she's here. I just spoke to the nurse about two hours ago when I landed in Seattle."

The woman sniffed and looked down at her computer again. "How do you spell that?"

"J-A-M-E-S-O-N." Alex clenched his jaw and prepared

to vault over the desk if she didn't hurry up and give him his grandmother's room number.

She stared at the computer for a few more seconds. "Here it is. She's in the Cardiac Care Unit, room 417. The elevator is just…"

He charged down the hall without waiting for the rest of her directions. He didn't like to be rude, especially to elderly women, but he had to find his grandmother and make sure she was all right.

He punched the up button and glared at the unmoving numbers above the elevator doors. Maybe he should take the stairs. But the elevator slid open, and he hustled in and punched the fourth-floor button.

Closing his eyes, he tried to slow his breathing and calm down. He had to prepare himself to see his grandmother. The nurse he'd spoken to said she'd had a heart attack. They weren't sure how much damage it had done. They were still running tests.

At least it had happened at the bakery when there were people around to help. What if she had collapsed at home when she was alone? If that had been the case, he would have gotten a very different kind of phone call.

He gritted his teeth and pushed that terrible thought away. Everything was going to be all right. This hospital had a great reputation. They would give his grandmother the best care possible. He'd make sure of it.

His thoughts rushed back to that morning and the frantic phone call he'd received from his old friend Annie Romano. It was strange that she had been the one to call. He thought she'd left Fairhaven after she graduated from high school. Apparently she'd come back.

His thoughts jumped back to the call. Hearing the ambulance siren wail in the background as Annie hurried through the story had shaken him to the core.

He could not lose his grandmother. She had raised him since he was twelve and seen him through the most difficult years of his life. She was the only family he had left.

The elevator doors opened on the fourth floor, and he hustled down the hall, scanning the room numbers as he went. The scent of hospital antiseptic lingered in the air, along with what smelled like meat loaf. He glanced at an uncovered dinner tray on the meal cart, and his empty stomach contracted. He hadn't eaten since breakfast.

"Alex?" a female voice called.

He turned, and his breath snagged in his throat. Annie Romano walked toward him…at least he thought it was Annie. She looked so different, he wasn't quite sure. But the long black curls cascading over her shoulders in shiny dark tendrils were the same.

"Hi, Annie." He gave her a brief hug. The comforting scent of brown sugar and vanilla floated around her. "Thanks for calling me."

"Of course."

He stepped back and glanced down the hall. "How's my grandmother?"

Annie followed his gaze. "They brought her upstairs from the E.R. a couple hours ago, but she was barely settled before they sent her off for another test."

That didn't sound good. Why were they still doing tests? He'd hoped she would be resting in her room and he could see her right away. He frowned and looked down the hall toward the nurses' station.

Annie gently touched his arm. "The nurse said she's stable and responding well to the medications. I think she's going to be all right." Unmistakable compassion filled her dark brown eyes.

Suddenly his throat felt too tight to speak. He nodded and quickly looked away.

Annie set her foam coffee cup on the end table in the visitors' lounge. "I haven't spoken to any of her doctors, but the nurses have been great."

He watched her, still taking in the changes in her appearance. People had teased her about being tall and slim when she was younger. She'd even been nicknamed Grasshopper. But that description certainly didn't fit anymore. Her navy jeans and red turtleneck couldn't hide her attractive figure.

He blew out a deep breath. Enough gawking already.

Annie pointed to her cup. "Would you like some coffee?"

The thought and aroma made his mouth water. "No, that's all right. You go ahead."

"Please." She smiled. "I didn't drink any yet." She reached for the cup and held it out to him.

"Okay. Thanks." He took a sip and let the warm drink soothe his tense nerves.

He heard approaching voices and glanced over his shoulder. Hannah Bodine, Marian Chandler and Barb Gunderson, three of his grandmother's closest friends, hurried toward them.

"Oh, Alex, I'm so glad you're here." Tears glistened in Hannah's eyes as she reached to hug him.

"Thanks, Hannah."

"As soon as Harry called and told me what happened, I called all the Treasures." Barb nodded toward Marian and Hannah.

Marian Chandler, owner of Bayside Books, clasped his hand. "We've all been praying. I know God's going to answer those prayers."

His grandmother and her three elderly friends were as close as sisters and affectionately known around town as the Bayside Treasures. For years they'd been meeting each week at Bayside Books to play Scrabble, share the latest news, and pray for friends and family.

"We couldn't just sit at home and wait for news," Barb said. "So I picked up the girls and we came over around noon."

"We've been here ever since, but we just took a little dinner break," Marian said, her pale face lined with concern.

Alex nodded. "I appreciate you coming, and I know Gram will, too."

"There's got to be something we can do besides just sit in the waiting room," Hannah said, getting teary-eyed again.

"Praying for her is a wonderful idea." Annie's soothing tone relieved some of the tension.

"You can count on us for that." Marian gave a decisive nod. "We'll be storming the heavens."

"I think I'll go talk to the nurses and see what I can find out." Alex set the coffee cup on the end table. "Maybe they'll give me more information since I'm family."

Annie's eyes widened, and she shot a quick look at the other women. They all exchanged nervous glances.

Barb cleared her throat. "Good idea. Maybe you'll be able to speak to the doctor."

He strode out of the visitors' lounge.

"Alex, wait." Annie hurried down the hall after him.

He turned and waited for her to catch up.

"There's something I need to tell you." She pressed her lips together, and her cheeks took on a rosy tint. "When I came to the hospital this morning, I told the nurse I was family."

He cocked his head and studied her.

"I'm sorry, but I was afraid they wouldn't let me see her if I said I was just a friend, and I didn't want her to be alone in the E.R." She looked up and met his gaze. "And then your grandma's friends got wind of it, and they all told the nurse they were her sisters."

He didn't know if he should be upset with them or laugh

at their crazy antics. Then his stomach tensed as the truth became clear. He was the only family member Gram had left, but he hadn't been here to help her when she needed him. Thank goodness her friends had stepped in.

"I know I've been away for a while," Annie continued, "but I've always thought of Irene as the closest thing I have to family in Fairhaven. I hope you're not upset with me."

A smile tugged at one corner of his mouth. How could he be upset? She'd bent a hospital rule, but she'd done it to comfort his grandmother. "No, it's okay. I know she thinks a lot of you."

"Well, Irene was always there for me." She clasped her hands tightly. "And no one should have to go through a frightening situation like this alone. I know what that's like, and I wouldn't wish it on anyone." She stopped. Her eyes widened, and she quickly looked away.

He wondered what she meant, but let that thought pass. "I'm glad you were there this morning." He reached out and touched her arm. "Thank you for helping her...and for everything."

Her smile returned. "You're welcome."

Looking into her dark brown eyes, the years seemed to fade, and memories of the friendship they'd shared as teenagers came flooding back. She'd been fifteen, and he eighteen when she started working at Jameson's. He treated her like a kid sister, teasing her about her braces and the way she always had her nose stuck in a book. But she'd been a good sport, and she'd even teased him back about his corny jokes and the fact that he was left-handed.

But when he was down, she was a great listener. Somehow she'd always get him to open up and say what was bothering him. And she never made him feel foolish for sharing it. That was something special he appreciated about Annie. She'd always had a compassionate heart.

Chapter Two

Annie glanced at her watch and hurried down the fourth-floor hall of St. Joseph's. She only had thirty minutes for this morning's visit with Irene, but at least she could drop off a little treat and check on her friend. Maybe she would even see Alex again. She quickly squelched that thought.

It would not be smart to fall for Alex Jameson, no matter how much the old attraction pulled her in that direction. Besides, she should not be thinking about getting involved with anyone. Launching her business, finding a part-time job and caring for her daughter had to be her priorities.

Even if he were interested in her, it would never work. Alex would be headed back to San Francisco soon, leaving her behind just as he had ten years ago. Slipping back into the pattern of wishing he would see her as more than a friend would only lead to heartache, and that was the last thing she needed.

A relationship with Alex would never work. She wouldn't let it.

The door of room 417 stood ajar. Annie knocked and waited.

"Come in." Irene's sweet reply made Annie smile.

She walked into the room and greeted Irene with a kiss on the cheek. "How are you feeling today?"

"Better, much better."

"That's good to hear."

"My, you certainly look lovely today. That red scarf really brings out the color in your cheeks."

"Thanks, Irene. You always say kind things."

"Well, it's true." Irene glanced at Annie's tote bag. "What did you bring me today?"

This was Irene's third day in the hospital, and Annie had surprised her with a gift and healthy snack each time she visited. "I brought you your own personal copy of the *Bellingham Herald* and some homemade applesauce." She placed the newspaper and plastic container on the bedside table.

"Oh, you're wonderful. I'm about to die from eating this hospital diet food." She grimaced and shuddered. "It's awful, truly awful."

"Well, it's not easy to prepare good-tasting, heart-healthy food in a large institutional kitchen."

"I know. I should just be grateful someone else is doing the cooking. But it's hard to eat plain oatmeal and drink coffee without sugar or cream." She sighed. "But the doctor says if I'm going to get better, I have to change my ways, especially my eating habits."

"Changes are challenging. But these are good changes, and they'll help you feel so much better."

"Good morning." Alex breezed in carrying a small arrangement of autumn-colored mums and peach roses. His thick dark hair was neatly combed but still looked slightly damp from his shower. He sent Annie a quick smile, then gave his grandmother a kiss on the forehead.

Annie's heart fluttered, and she quickly hid her reaction. Just because she'd had a crush on Alex when she was fifteen didn't mean she had to make a fool of herself each time he walked into the room.

"These flowers are beautiful." Irene leaned forward and sniffed. "They smell wonderful." She reached up and patted Alex's cheek. "You're spoiling me."

"You deserve to be spoiled." He set the flowers on the windowsill. "Did you talk to the doctor this morning?"

Irene nodded. "He said I might be able to go home tomorrow or Saturday if my blood work comes back okay, and I promise to follow all his instructions."

Alex nodded and crossed his arms. "And of course you will."

A worried frown settled on Irene's face. "The nurse and a nutritionist came in earlier and gave me a stack of booklets about diet and exercise." She took one from the bedside table, and her face flushed. "I can't eat anything from the bakery—no breads, no muffins, no cookies, no potatoes and no pasta."

"Lean protein, vegetables and fruit are all okay. Whole grains like brown rice and quinoa are usually on the list, too." Annie hoped that would encourage her friend, but Irene's anxious expression didn't ease.

"I'm supposed to rest several times a day and avoid lifting, but it says I need to exercise and not overdo it." The booklet shook in her trembling hand. "How am I supposed to make sense of all this?"

Getting upset couldn't be good for Irene's heart. Annie sent Alex a warning glance.

Understanding flashed in his blue eyes, and he laid his hand on his grandmother's arm. "I know it all seems overwhelming right now, but I'll help you figure it out."

"How are you going to do that? You have to go back to San Francisco soon." Irene clamped her lips together and turned away from Alex.

"I've got two weeks' vacation plus Thanksgiving weekend, and I can ask for more time off if I need it. But that should be long enough to line up some help and be sure you're settled at home."

"What I need is someone to read all these silly things and tell me what to do." Irene waved her hand at the booklets. Her chin began to quiver, and tears flooded her eyes. "I'm sorry. I don't know why I'm getting so emotional." She sniffed and snatched a tissue from the small box on her bedside table.

"It's all right, Gram," Alex said, his voice low and husky. "I know this has been hard for you."

"It's all my fault," she continued as though she hadn't heard Alex. "I've been working too hard and not taking good care of myself." Her tears overflowed and spilled down her pale, wrinkled cheeks. "The good Lord gave me lots of warnings, but I ignored them."

Annie took Irene's hand, her heart aching for her friend. Guilt and regret were feelings she understood all too well. "You always told me to take my problems to the Lord. Have you talked to Him about this?"

She exhaled a shuddering sigh. "I had a good prayer time this morning and confessed it all. I know He forgives me. I guess I'm just feeling sorry for myself now." She wiped her nose with a tissue.

Annie squeezed Irene's hand. "You can't change the past, but you can learn from it and make better choices for the future." She sent Irene an encouraging smile. "That's what you need to focus on now—your future."

Alex took his grandmother's other hand. "That's right. And I'll be here to help you get back on your feet. Soon you'll be feeling better and enjoying life again."

The nurse walked in. "Morning, everyone. It's time for me to help Mrs. Jameson with a few things." She lifted her eyebrows and added a pointed look.

Annie gave Irene a gentle hug and stepped back. "I'll call you later and see how you're doing."

Alex kissed Irene's cheek, promised to return that afternoon, then said goodbye and walked with Annie out of the room and headed toward the elevator.

"Annie, I've been thinking, and I have something I want to ask you."

She looked up, surprised by his serious tone. "Sure. What is it?"

"My grandmother needs someone to help her when she comes home, and I know you're a chef, so I was wondering—"

"I'd love to make some meals for her. I learned how to cook according to the American Heart Association guidelines at culinary school."

He nodded, but his somber expression didn't change. "Meals would be helpful. But what I'm really looking for is someone to live with her and help her at home until she recovers."

She thought about that for a moment, then slowly shook her head. "I'm sorry, Alex. I'd love to stay with Irene, but I have a business to run and a daughter to support."

His eyebrows rose. "A daughter?"

Her stomach clenched. She thought he knew about Emma. But it made sense that he didn't. Irene wasn't one to spread gossip about Annie, and apparently Alex didn't come home to Fairhaven often enough to hear it from someone else. Even if he had, why would anyone mention her situation to him? She was just a former employee who went off to college, got on the wrong track and found herself in a whole lot of trouble.

Slipping her hands in her jacket pockets, she pushed those painful thoughts away. It didn't matter now. She'd made her choices, and she had to live with them.

She looked up and met his curious gaze. "Yes, I have a

five-year-old daughter, Emma." There was so much more
to the story, but she wasn't sure if he wanted to hear it, or if
she had the courage to tell him.

He nodded and rubbed his chin. "Does she go to school?"

"Yes, she's in kindergarten."

"So you're free during the day?"

For an intelligent guy, he sure didn't seem to get the picture. "No. I'm not free. I work as a personal chef." The elevator doors slid open and they stepped in.

"Okay. Fill me in. What does a personal chef do?"

"I meet with clients at their homes and discuss their food
preferences and meal needs. Then I plan the menus, do the
shopping and go back to their homes to cook several meals
at one time."

He nodded. "Sounds like a smart business plan."

"It's great for people who want healthy, home-cooked
meals but for various reasons don't want to do it themselves."

"Do you cook for a lot of people?"

She shrugged one shoulder, not wanting to admit how few
clients she'd lined up in the past two months. "I'm doing a
lot of networking right now, getting the word out."

His intense gaze remained focused on her.

She blew out a deep breath. "Okay, the truth is, I'm just
getting started, and I only have two weekly clients. The day
Irene collapsed, I'd gone to the bakery to ask her for a part-
time job."

He nodded, a slight smile pulling up one side of his mouth.

Was he glad she'd been honest, or just happy that she
might be free to help him?

"So why not take the job caring for my grandmother?"

Surprise rippled through her. "You want to hire me?"

"Yes. I wasn't expecting you to do it for free."

She gave an embarrassed little chuckle. "Sorry, I didn't
understand what you meant."

"I guess I didn't explain it very well." He sent her a sheepish smile. "So what do you say? Would you be willing to move in with my grandmother and oversee her meals and home care?"

The elevator reached the first floor, and the doors opened, giving her a moment to think. Could she afford to put her fledgling business on hold to help Irene? Would that be wise? What about Emma? How would Irene deal with having a five-year-old in her house when she was recovering from a heart attack?

He followed her out of the elevator. "There's plenty of room at the house for you and your daughter. You could have those two bedrooms on the first floor. I'd move my stuff upstairs."

She pulled in a sharp breath. "You're staying there, too?"

"Just until we've got everything settled with her care and I figure out what to do with the bakery."

Her steps stalled. "You are going to keep the bakery open, aren't you?"

"I'm not sure. Harry has been running things since Gram's heart attack, but it doesn't sound like it's going very well."

"You can't close. Your grandmother loves that shop. Her staff and customers are like family to her."

"I know…but I've got to think of what's best for her health now." Lines creased his forehead. "And I've got to find someone to stay with her when she comes home from the hospital."

She pressed her lips together, still debating her answer.

"Annie?" He softened his tone, and the way he said her name sent shivers up her arms.

"Yes?"

He fixed his deep blue gaze on her again. "It would be a huge help if you could take care of her. I know she'd feel comfortable with you there, not just because you can cook healthy meals, but because she considers you a friend."

Annie's heart fluttered. *Oh, my goodness.* Alex Jameson was even more charming than he'd been ten years ago. If she wasn't careful, she'd find herself right back where she'd been at fifteen—lonely and heartbroken as she watched him walk out the door and leave her behind.

She cleared her throat as she took a step back. "I want to help, but I need some more time to think it through before I make a decision."

"Okay." His shoulders sagged slightly. "But I need to find someone right away, so I'd appreciate you letting me know as soon as possible."

The scent of freshly perked coffee and warm apple-cider doughnuts drifted toward Alex as he stepped into the bakery. His mouth watered, and his empty stomach rumbled. How long had it been since he'd had one of those cinnamon-and-sugar-dusted treats? Too long.

"Hey there!" Harry came around the end of the counter and gripped Alex's hand. "Good to see you, Alex. How's Irene doing?" The aging baker wore a WWU Vikings baseball cap and long white apron with a few splotches of what looked like chocolate frosting on the bib.

"She seems a little stronger each day. The doctor said she might be coming home tomorrow." He smiled. "And you know she's happy about that."

Harry chuckled. "I can imagine."

"I really appreciate you taking charge."

"We're doing our best to keep things going." Harry glanced around the shop, a concerned look in his eyes. "This place means a lot to Irene. Sure would hate to see it close."

Alex nodded and scanned the shop's shabby interior. "Looks like the place could use a little TLC to brighten things up."

"Yeah, I suppose so. Maybe you could give us a hand. How long are you going to be in town?"

"I'll be here through Thanksgiving weekend."

"We could get a lot done by then."

Alex frowned at the flickering fluorescent light overhead. He hadn't done any hands-on repair work since he left Fairhaven, and he wasn't sure he wanted to spend his vacation fixing up the bakery. "I'll talk to my grandmother about hiring someone."

Harry clicked his tongue. "I'm not sure she can afford it."

Alex straightened. "Really?"

Harry nodded. "Things have changed around here, Alex, especially since your grandpa passed away."

Alex had no idea his grandmother's business was struggling. "So you don't think she can afford to pay someone to do the work?"

Harry shrugged. "She's the one paying the bills, but these past few months she's been cutting Janelle's and Clyde's hours and covering the extra shifts herself." He pushed up the brim of his cap. "Do you think that could've caused the heart attack?"

Alex clenched his hands in his pockets. "I don't know, but a woman her age shouldn't be on her feet all day, trying to run a business like this."

"I've been telling her she needs to slow down and let us carry more of the load. But she kept telling me not to worry."

"She's a hard worker. She always has been. And she doesn't like to admit she can't do everything she used to."

"I'm afraid you're right about that."

Alex crossed his arms and studied the peeling paint around the front windows and the cracked floor tiles. It was time he had a frank discussion with his grandmother about the future of the bakery. He hated to think of closing Jameson's or putting it up for sale, but what other options did they have?

Twenty minutes later Alex drove through town, heading back to his grandmother's house. The trouble at the bakery and the pressing need to find someone to stay with his grandmother buzzed through his mind.

Annie would be perfect for the job. She could cook for Gram and teach her how to make healthy meals. That would be a huge switch for his grandmother. The woman practically had chocolate frosting running through her veins, but that was no longer an option, not if she was going to recover and prevent another heart attack.

There must be some way he could convince Annie to say yes. Maybe if he gave her a call and shared the salary he had in mind… He could even up it a few hundred if she was on the fence. Surely his grandmother had savings that would cover the expense.

As he pulled in the driveway, his cell phone rang. He took it from his pocket and checked the screen.

Tiffany Charles. Why was she calling? Likely some problem at work. Didn't they realize he was dealing with a family crisis? He stifled an irritated huff and answered the call.

"I thought you'd want to hear the latest rumor going around."

"Okay. What's up?"

"Jenifer said she heard Tremont and Sellers talking about a possible merger."

"You're kidding."

"No. Not this time."

"With who? Hilton? Wyndham?"

"They didn't say."

"Did she get any more details?"

"Just that they're expecting an offer soon."

"An offer? That means someone's probably buying us out, not the other way around."

"That's what it sounds like." Silence buzzed along the line for a few seconds. "Alex, this is not a good time for you to be away."

"I know, but I don't really have a choice."

"So when are you coming back?"

"Probably not until after Thanksgiving."

Tiffany groaned. "Everyone is going crazy down here trying to do their own work and cover for you."

He scowled and shook his head. She knew why he'd flown home to Fairhaven, but not once had she asked him how Gram was doing. "Look, Tiffany, my grandmother had a heart attack. I have two weeks' vacation coming. I need to be here."

She clicked her tongue. "You don't have to get huffy. I just thought you'd want to know what's going on."

He swallowed his irritation. "I appreciate the info."

"You should come back as soon as you can. All our jobs could be on the line."

"I understand." He pulled in a deep breath, added a quick thanks and ended the call. With a weary sigh, he climbed out of the car, trudged across the walk and up the porch steps.

Being single and living so far from his grandmother, he didn't usually have to worry about balancing his job and family. But things were different now. His grandmother needed him, and he wasn't going to let her down. No matter how much pressure Tiffany or anyone else from Tremont put on him, he was staying in Fairhaven until he was certain his grandmother was going to be okay. They'd just have to find a way to deal with things until he got back.

Annie paced across the apartment and looked out the window at the twinkling, star-studded sky. The beauty of the evening lifted her sagging spirit and gave her courage to follow through on her decision.

Emma was safely tucked into bed. It was time to make the call. She took her cell phone from her pocket and searched for Alex's number in her contacts list. Biting her lip, she tapped the screen and lifted the phone to her ear. After the second ring, Alex answered, his voice deep and melodic.

Her hand trembled slightly. "Hi, Alex. It's Annie. I was wondering if you found anyone to stay with Irene when she comes home from the hospital."

Silence hung between them for an extra second. "Not yet."

She swallowed, praying she wasn't making a mistake. "I'm interested. Could we get together and talk about it?"

"Okay. Great. The doctor says Gram will be coming home Saturday afternoon. Could you meet me at the house tomorrow morning, say eight-thirty?"

Annie's stomach clenched. Already she was going to have to negotiate. "Nine would be better for me. I have to drop Emma off at school at eight-forty-five."

"Hmm. Okay, nine o'clock." His voice had definitely cooled a few degrees.

Irritation flashed through her. "I want to help Irene, but my daughter has to be my first priority. If you're not willing to change the time of our meeting to accommodate her schedule—"

"That's not what I said."

"But that's what I heard in your voice."

"I was just thinking through my plan for the day. I wasn't implying anything negative about you or your daughter."

"Oh. Sorry."

"I told Harry I'd come by the bakery tomorrow before ten, but I can change that if we need to."

"No, I can be there by nine, maybe a little earlier." She walked back toward the kitchen, debating the wisdom of her next question, but she had to ask. "Do you think I'd still be able to do some work as a personal chef while I'm caring for Irene? I'd like to keep those two weekly clients if possible."

"We can talk about that when we get together tomorrow. I'll give you as much information as possible, and I'll expect you to be clear with me about your schedule and needs. Then we'll see if this job is a good fit for you." His voice was calm and steady, as though he negotiated deals and hired and fired people all the time. That didn't surprise her. Irene had told her he was a high-powered marketing and sales manager for a big hotel chain based in San Francisco.

She felt foolish now for jumping to conclusions about his tone of voice. If she wanted this job, she had better show flexibility and appreciation.

She straightened her shoulders. "Thanks for changing the time for me. I'll see you tomorrow at nine o'clock." She ended the call and dropped the phone in her pocket. With a weary shake of her head, she walked back toward the window once more.

Are You listening, Lord? Am I making the right choice? I prayed for a job, and this door opened, so I'm walking through it. Please watch over us, and if this is not the right path, please shut the door.

Chapter Three

Annie pulled into the driveway at Irene's late Saturday morning and let the motor idle. The large craftsman-style house, with its dark tan siding, stout white pillars and wide front porch, looked warm and welcoming. Bright orange mums filled large pots on the porch steps. Golden birch and maple leaves dotted the spacious front lawn. Still she hesitated to turn off the car.

"Is this where we're gonna stay?" Emma asked from the backseat.

Annie looked over her shoulder. "Yes, this is Mrs. Jameson's house. Isn't it pretty? Look at the cute pumpkins on her porch." For her daughter's sake, she forced lightness into her voice.

Emma leaned forward and looked out the window. She scanned the house and yard, apprehension in her eyes. Annie wished she could say more to reassure her daughter, but the words didn't come. Since they had arrived in Fairhaven in late August, they'd stayed with two different friends while Annie focused on starting her business. This new, temporary home would mean another adjustment for Emma.

"Okay, sweetie, let's go."

Emma released a sigh and climbed out while Annie grabbed her suitcase from the backseat.

The front door opened, and Alex walked down the porch steps. "Good morning," he called.

"Morning." Annie's hand trembled slightly as she clutched the suitcase. She had to stop having this silly reaction every time he was around.

"Here, let me get that for you." He reached past her.

"No. It's okay. I can get it." She wrestled the large piece of luggage out of the car.

He looked in and searched the empty backseat. "You fit all your clothes in one suitcase?" He grinned. "You're an amazing packer."

"Most of our things are in storage."

Emma peeked around the back of the car and studied Alex with a worried expression.

"Emma has a suitcase in the trunk. Maybe you could lift that out for her."

"Sure."

Annie followed him behind the car. "Emma, this is Alex. He's Mrs. Jameson's grandson."

She looked up at him and wrinkled her brow. "Grandson? He looks too old for that."

"Well, it's true. I'm her grandson. And you must be Emma." He leaned down and extended his hand.

Emma slowly reached out and grasped his fingers.

He winked and gave her hand a playful shake. "It's nice to meet you, Emma. I hope you and your mom will feel at home here."

Emma shot her mother a questioning look. Annie nodded, encouraging her to reply.

"Thanks." Emma sent him a shy smile, then dropped his hand and pointed to the trunk. "That's my suitcase."

"Okay." Alex hoisted the small red suitcase out and extended the handle. "Would you like me to take it for you?"

Emma shook her head. "No, I can do it."

Alex glanced at Annie with a slight smile.

She bit her lip, not missing the way Emma's response echoed her own.

With a determined tilt of her chin, Emma grabbed the handle and pulled the suitcase along the stone walkway. When she reached the front steps, Alex carried it up to the porch and then opened the front door for them.

Annie stepped through the doorway and into the entry. As she looked around the cozy living room and dining room, memories came flooding back.

She'd never forget the delicious meals Irene had prepared or the conversation and laughter they'd all shared around the table.

Irene and her husband, John, had always made her feel welcome, as if she was part of the family. And Alex had usually been there, too, with some of his friends from the basketball team—at least until he left for college.

"Annie?"

She spun around. "Sorry, I was just remembering how I used to come here when I was a teenager."

"Happy memories, I hope."

"Yes, very happy. Remember how we used to play Scrabble with your grandparents?"

He nodded, his blue gaze growing more intense. "Those were good times."

Her face warmed, and she swallowed. "Yes, they were."

Another second passed before he looked away. "Well, I imagine you'd like to get settled." He led the way down the hall. "My grandmother's room is here." He pointed to the first door on the right. "I thought you'd like to have the room next door."

Annie followed him in and looked around. A queen-size bed covered with a beautiful handmade quilt in sage-green and lavender filled the center of the room. A whitewashed oak dresser with an oval mirror stood against the opposite wall. White eyelet curtains tied back with lavender ribbons hung over the two windows. And in the corner sat a pretty sage-green overstuffed chair with a small round table and lamp next to it. It looked like a cozy spot where she could read her Bible in the morning.

Irene had added several homey touches to the room—two African violets on the windowsill, a whitewashed basket of magazines by the chair and a loosely woven lavender throw on the end of the bed, along with plenty of plump decorative pillows.

"Oh, this is lovely."

"Glad you like it."

"Where am I going to sleep?" Emma asked.

"You have your own room right across the hall. Come on. I'll show you."

Annie dropped off her suitcase and followed Alex and Emma.

"Here you go." Alex opened the door, and they stepped into Emma's new room. It was decorated in red, white and navy blue and had pine, country-style furniture that included two twin beds and a tall dresser and mirror. A large wooden rocker and antique trunk sat in one corner. A window seat with a padded cushion and pillows looked like the perfect spot for Emma to sit and daydream or read a picture book.

"I usually stay in here, so I can vouch for the bed being very comfortable." He gave the closest twin bed a pat and smiled at Emma.

Her daughter parked her rolling suitcase and reached for

the patchwork cat that sat by the pillows at the head of the bed. "What's his name?"

Alex rubbed his chin. "I'm not sure he has one."

Emma's eyes widened, and she looked at him as if that was unbelievable.

"Emma usually names all her stuffed animals."

"Oh, well, maybe you should name him."

Emma touched the cat's black button eyes and red collar, obviously giving it some thought. "His name is...Charlie."

Alex nodded. "Then Charlie it is."

"Who's going to sleep over there?" Emma pointed to the other twin bed.

"I suppose Charlie can sleep there, unless you want him to sleep with you."

Emma smiled and hugged the cat to her chest.

Annie's heart warmed as she watched her daughter. Maybe staying with Irene and Alex would work out after all. Perhaps they'd even found a place where they could settle in and feel at home...at least for a while.

Alex's cell phone chirped in his pocket. He pulled it out. "That's my alarm. Time for me to head down to the hospital and pick up Gram."

Annie lifted one eyebrow.

Did he always use an alarm like that? He slipped his phone back in his pocket. "Make yourself at home. There's some leftover pizza in the kitchen if you're hungry. We should be back no later than four o'clock."

"Thanks." Annie began thinking through dinner menus as he gave Emma a smile and a light pat on the head, then headed out the bedroom door.

Emma's gaze followed him as he disappeared around the corner. "He's nice." She cuddled the cat in her arms and leaned back against the side of the bed.

"Yes. He is," Annie said and released a soft sigh.

* * *

Later that afternoon, Alex opened the passenger door and helped his grandmother out of the car. She turned and reached for her tote bag.

"Let me get that for you, Gram."

"I've got it."

"But the doctor said you're not supposed to lift things."

"It's just a tote bag."

He took hold of the bag's handle, and she released it with a resigned sigh.

"I wished you'd stop fussing over me, Alex. I'm going to be fine."

"Of course you are, but you've got to follow the doctor's instructions to the letter." That's why he planned to stay through Thanksgiving, to make sure his grandmother accepted those changes and obeyed the doctor's orders. That was the only way he'd have any peace of mind when he returned to San Francisco.

"If that tote bag is heavy, it's because it's full of all those directions from that doctor."

He studied her expression and read the anxiety in her eyes. "It's okay, Gram. We'll sort through them and make a plan."

"You and your plans." Her expression more at ease, she tucked her hand into the crook of his arm and they walked up the stone pathway toward the house. They slowly mounted the steps.

She was weaker than he'd realized. Once again the possibility of losing her hit him. He clenched his jaw, fighting off those thoughts.

He ushered her inside. The delicious scent of dinner cooking drifted out from the kitchen. He pulled in a deep breath, and some of the tightness in his neck and shoulders eased.

"Something smells wonderful," Irene said as she unbuttoned her coat.

"Here, let me help you." Alex slipped her coat off and hung it in the front closet.

Emma rushed around the corner from the dining room with the patchwork cat tucked under one arm and a piece of notebook paper with red marker scribbled all over it in the other. "Mom, they're here," she called in a surprisingly loud voice for a five-year-old.

Irene smiled. "You must be Emma."

She nodded and held out the paper to Gram. "I made this for you."

"Why, thank you, dear." She pushed her glasses up her nose and examined the paper. "Tell me all about it."

Emma came closer. "This is your house," she said, pointing to the rectangle in the middle. "And this is me and my mom, and that's Charlie." She held out the patchwork cat.

"Ah, yes, Charlie. I see." Gram looked up and grinned at him, apparently delighted with the greeting and drawing.

Annie stepped out from the kitchen wearing a white apron over her red turtleneck and black pants. She'd tied her hair back, and her cheeks were flushed pink. "Welcome home." She gave Irene a quick hug.

"What are you cooking, dear? It smells wonderful."

Annie's eyes brightened. "I made grilled chicken with pineapple-and-mango salsa, brown rice and asparagus."

"Oh, that sounds delicious, especially after all that cardboard hospital food."

Alex looked past her. "You found all that in the kitchen?"

"No. Emma and I made a little run to the grocery store."

"Keep your receipts, and I'll refund you."

She nodded. "I picked up a few basics for breakfast and lunch. But we can sit down tonight or tomorrow and plan the week's menu."

Gram stepped forward and pulled her in for a tight hug. "Thank you, Annie. I'm so glad you're here."

Annie closed her eyes, looking as though she enjoyed the hug as much as his grandmother. "Me, too." She glanced down at Emma. "We're both glad, aren't we, Em?"

Emma nodded, and her dark curls bounced. "I like your house."

Gram chuckled. "Well, thank you." She looked around. "I like it, too, especially after spending five days in the hospital."

Alex slipped his arm around Gram's shoulder. "We're all happy you're home."

Annie blinked a couple times and sent them a tremulous smile. "I need a few more minutes to finish cooking dinner."

"Take your time, dear. I think I'd like to just sit down for a bit and look through the mail."

Alex took his grandmother's arm and led her to her favorite recliner. "Why don't you just relax and put your feet up until dinner?"

She settled into her chair. "Would you bring me the mail?"

"Sure." He retrieved the stack from the desk in the dining room, and as he passed the table, he noticed Annie had set only two places for dinner.

He brought Gram the mail, then headed for the kitchen. Emma sat at the table, coloring with a bright purple marker. At least a dozen drawings lay scattered across the big pine table.

Annie stood at the counter chopping chunks of fresh pineapple. She looked up as he crossed the kitchen.

"How come you only set two places at the table?"

She looked down and kept chopping. "Emma and I can eat in here."

"But I thought you would eat with us. I mean, you're welcome to eat with us…unless you'd rather eat out here. But that doesn't really make sense." He wasn't sure why he was stumbling over his words.

"It's okay, Alex." Her dark-eyed gaze flashed toward him and then darted away. "I'm the employee now. It's different than before. I understand."

His heart clenched. "Annie, look at me."

She slowly turned. The vulnerability in her eyes cut through him.

"I might be paying you to cook and take care of Gram, but we were friends first. That hasn't changed."

"You don't have to do this, Alex."

"Do what?"

"Be so nice."

"Inviting you to sit down and have dinner with us—a dinner that you cooked—that's your definition of nice?"

Her lips curved into a small smile. "I guess so."

He crossed to the cabinet and took out two more plates. "Then you are about to be treated to a very nice dinner."

Her smile spread wider. "Thank you, Alex."

His chest expanded as he took two more sets of silverware from the drawer. Annie Romano deserved a place at the table, and he was going to make sure she got it. He didn't want her to feel as if she was just an employee.

She was much more than that. She always had been.

Chapter Four

Annie stirred the chopped apples into the bubbling oats and lowered the heat. Just five more minutes and breakfast would be ready.

The coffee was brewing. The table was set. Alex and Irene were both up and getting ready for the day.

Where was Emma? She'd sent her off to put on her shoes at least ten minutes ago, but she hadn't returned.

If this were her own house, she'd call out and give her daughter a five-minute warning, but she didn't have that freedom here. Instead, she set aside the wooden spoon and walked down the hall in search of her daughter.

Emma's door stood open. Annie looked in and found her sitting on the floor with pieces of a large puzzle spread out around her on the rug.

"Emma, what are you doing? I sent you in here to get your shoes, remember?"

Her daughter looked up. "I couldn't find 'um."

"Well…where did you leave them?"

She blinked her big brown eyes and shrugged. "I don't know." Her daughter had a terrible time keeping track of things, and moving from place to place made it difficult to reinforce the helpful routines she needed—like putting away her shoes.

"Where were you when you took them off?"

Emma glanced around. "I don't 'member."

Whispering a prayer for patience, Annie held out her hand to Emma. "Okay. Let's go on a shoe hunt."

Her daughter slowly rose and took her hand. They spent the next few minutes searching Emma's room, but the shoes were not there. Then they checked the bathroom. No shoes.

"Did you take them off in here?" Annie pushed open her bedroom door.

"Maybe." Emma chewed on her thumbnail as she walked around. Suddenly she gasped and dropped to her knees. Lifting the bed skirt, she peeked underneath. "Here they are!"

"Good job." Annie gave her a pat on the back. "Hop up on the bed, and I'll give you a hand."

Emma climbed up and sat on the edge. Annie knelt and slipped on the shoes. "I want you to keep these shoes on your feet or in your room. No more taking them off and just leaving them lying—"

"Annie!" Alex called as he hustled past her door. "Something is burning!"

Annie gasped. "The oatmeal!" She ran down the hall after him. How could she have forgotten she'd left it simmering on the stove? What was the matter with her?

Alex reached the kitchen first. A hazy gray cloud hung in the air, carrying the scent of scorched oats. He grabbed the smoking pot, jerked open the back door and strode outside.

"Was that breakfast?" Emma asked in a small voice.

"Yes," Annie said with a shudder. She snatched a kitchen towel and waved it through the air, trying to move the smoke outside.

Irene walked into the kitchen. "What's burning?"

Annie's face flamed. "The oats." She turned to Irene.

"I'm sorry. I went to get Emma, and she couldn't find her shoes. We had to look all over the house." She opened the window above the sink. Cool air rushed in. "I can't believe I did that. I know better than to walk away and leave something cooking on the stove."

"I should hope so." Alex shoved the back door closed with a bang. "Seems like that would be the first lesson in Cooking 101."

"Alex." Irene sent him a stern glance. "Annie apologized. There's no need to scold her. It was an accident."

"An accident that could've been avoided if she wasn't distracted by…" His gaze dipped to Emma.

Annie's stomach clenched, and she laid a protective hand on Emma's shoulder. Her daughter looked up at her with a hint of fear in her large brown eyes.

Annie shot Alex a heated glance, then looked down at her daughter. "It's all right, Emma."

Irene nodded to Alex, as though prompting him to apologize.

His expression eased a bit. "I'm sorry. I just wasn't expecting our breakfast to go up in smoke."

Annie clamped her mouth closed, turned away and took a pot from the cabinet. "I'll start another batch." She'd have to use the old-fashioned rolled oats rather than the steel cut.

"Don't make any for me," Alex said, his voice still carrying a measure of irritation. "I need to get going. I'm covering for Harry at the bakery this morning."

"Why did he need the morning off?" Irene asked.

"I don't know, Gram. He didn't say."

"Maybe I should give him a call." Irene walked toward the phone.

Alex laid his hand on her shoulder. "Please, Gram, you don't need to call. I'll take care of things at the bakery. You just focus on getting better."

"But it's been a long time since you worked there. Are you sure you know how to handle things?"

"I'm just manning the counter. I'm sure it'll all come back to me."

"All right, but promise you'll call me if you have any questions."

"Don't worry. I'll call."

Annie poured the oats into the pan. "Are you sure you don't have time for breakfast? These only take five minutes."

"No. I'll just grab something at the bakery." He sent her one more serious look, then turned and walked out of the kitchen.

Irene watched him go, then shook her head. "I have a feeling he's not telling me something."

"Why do you say that?"

"It's not like him to get so upset about a scorched pan of oatmeal."

Annie walked to the sink and filled a measuring cup with water. Was Irene right? Was something else besides the burnt breakfast bothering Alex?

Looking out the window, she watched him climb into his grandmother's car and back out of the driveway.

She didn't like to disappoint Alex—especially since she'd just started working for him. But it was more than just not wanting to let down her employer.

Alex was much more than that. He always had been.

Alex slammed the car door and glared at himself in the rearview mirror. What was wrong with him? Why had he flown off the handle at Annie like that? It was just a stupid pot of oatmeal, not a major disaster. He jerked the car in Reverse and backed out of the driveway, tires squealing as he drove away.

She probably thought he was a real grouch—and she was right.

But burnt breakfast wasn't the real reason for his rotten mood. The phone calls he'd received earlier that morning were the real trigger that set off his stormy reaction.

First Harry had called to report more problems at the bakery. And less than five minutes later, Tiffany phoned with the news that someone had leaked the possible merger to the press. Now everyone at Tremont was texting and exchanging panicked emails. Tiffany predicted heads would roll, and not just the head of the person who had leaked the story.

Acidic coffee sloshed in his empty stomach and burned his throat. The troubles at work and at the bakery were enough to give him a permanent stomachache, but the memories of Annie's reaction to his harsh words made him feel even worse. He'd seen that look of betrayal in her eyes. She deserved better from him.

He pulled to a stop at the corner, wrestling to get that image out of his mind. But the weight of conviction felt like a heavy hand pressing down on his shoulders.

"All right. I'll apologize to Annie as soon as I get back to Gram's."

He wasn't sure who he was talking to, but with that decision made, the weight seemed to lift a bit, and he could focus on the issues at work.

He didn't have the power to change the situation at Tremont. But he could shoot off an email to a few of his friends at work to try to put out some fires. What would he say? If the company was sold, they might all lose their jobs, and in this economy finding a new one wouldn't be easy. But maybe they were all worried for nothing. Only time would tell.

He rounded the corner at Eleventh and Harris, spotted an open parking place and pulled in.

Walking toward the bakery, he looked at the other buildings. Their neat brick-and-wood exteriors were a stark contrast to the bakery's faded and outdated appearance. Jameson's really needed a face-lift—or at least a paint job to spruce it up.

But could Gram afford that?

It was time to find out.

Annie scrubbed the oatmeal pan with steel wool, trying to remove the last burnt marks. She'd let it soak for several hours, hoping that would make the job easier, but it hadn't done much good.

Lifting her arm, she brushed a stray curl off her damp forehead. Only three days into this new arrangement with Alex, and she already doubted she'd made the right decision.

Everything had started off okay. Alex seemed to appreciate having her here, but the first time she'd made a mistake, he'd shown his true colors. Irritation rose, and her face flamed. Hadn't he ever burned something on the stove? Didn't he ever get distracted and forget things?

She huffed. Probably not. He was always on schedule, setting a constant alarm to keep him that way.

Well, he didn't have a five-year-old daughter or half the responsibilities she carried every day.

Thank goodness he wasn't staying here permanently. The sooner she could convince him she had things under control, the sooner he'd return to San Francisco. And today was not soon enough for her.

A car pulled in the driveway. Alex climbed out and shut the door.

Her stomach tensed. Irene was resting, and she had at least another hour before she had to pick up Emma from school. She quickly rinsed the pot and set it in the dish drainer to dry. Hopefully Alex had calmed down and wouldn't mention the burnt breakfast.

He walked in the back door carrying a large cardboard box. His steps slowed when he spotted her at the sink. "Hi, Annie."

"Hello." She turned away and wiped the counter.

"Where's Gram?"

"She's taking a nap." She tossed the paper towel in the trash can and turned to face him.

He set the box on the counter. A slight frown creased his forehead. "Listen…I was thinking about what happened this morning, and I realize I overreacted." He slipped his hands in his pants pockets. "I'm sorry."

She stared at him for a second before she could put a sentence together. "You don't have to apologize to me."

"Yes, I do. I shouldn't be taking my frustration out on you."

"Well, I can see how starting the day with a burnt breakfast would be frustrating."

"That was a surprise, but I got a phone call before that, which is what really set me off. But that's not your fault."

Annie's heart warmed and softened. "Who called?"

He glanced toward the hallway. "I don't want Gram to hear this."

"I just checked on her a few minutes ago. She's sound asleep." Annie motioned toward the table. "Do you want to have some coffee?"

"Sure." He pulled out a chair and sat down.

"So someone called?" She took a mug from the cabinet.

"Yeah, Harry said the big Hobart mixer came to a grinding halt this morning."

"Oh, no."

"That's what I said." They used that mixer for everything from bread dough to cake batter.

She poured him a cup of coffee and took out a tin of gingersnaps from the pantry. No wonder he was upset. Sympathy flowed through her as she carried the coffee to the table and sat down across from him.

"I just spent the last few hours looking over the finances at the bakery." He nodded toward the container on the counter by the back door. "I brought home a big stack of bills and files."

"How do things look?"

"Harry and I tried to make sense of it, but I'm going to need Gram's help to figure out her system."

"I hope that won't upset her."

"We don't really have a choice. I have to get a clear picture of the income and expenses so we can make a decision about the future of the bakery." He set his coffee cup on the table. "But I'll be honest. It doesn't look good. Without that mixer, we can't keep up with our regular output, which means less income."

"Can you get the mixer repaired?"

"Maybe. I've got a call in to a company that sends out repairmen, but I'm not sure if Gram can afford that."

"Oh, Alex, is it really that bad?"

"I don't know…but Harry says Gram has been cutting her employees' hours. It also looks like she's been putting off paying some of the bills."

Annie sat back in her chair. Irene had said business was slow, but she had no idea things were this bad.

Irene strolled into the kitchen wearing brown plush pants, a matching pullover and fuzzy pink slippers. "Hey, you two, why the long faces?"

Annie's gaze darted to Alex.

Understanding flashed in his eyes, and he gave her a slight nod. "We were just talking, Gram."

Irene smiled, her brown eyes glowing. "Talking is good. Very good." She joined them at the table.

Annie's cheeks burned. She looked down and stirred her coffee. This was not the first time Irene had hinted at matchmaking hopes for her and Alex.

Alex smiled at his grandmother and seemed unaware of her hints. "Did you have a good nap?"

Gram nodded. "I can't believe I slept for almost two hours." She shook her head. "I'm getting awfully lazy."

"Well, you deserve to take it easy, Gram. You've worked hard all your life. Now it's time to get into a new routine and take good care of yourself."

"That's right," Annie said. "Resting each day is important for your recovery. It needs to be a priority."

Alex gave a decisive nod. "I couldn't have said it better myself."

Irene cocked her head and looked back and forth between them. "All right, you two. What's going on?"

Alex's eyes widened. "What do you mean?"

"You forget, Alex Jameson, I raised you. I can sense when you're not telling me something." Irene drilled them with her steady gaze. "Come on. Out with it."

"It's nothing for you to worry about, Gram."

"Well, I'm going to worry unless you tell me."

Alex got up from the table and poured himself a second cup of coffee. "Okay, but you have to promise you won't let it upset you."

"I promise."

Alex sat at the table again. "I spent some time at the bakery today. Harry and I made a list of the repairs that need to be made."

"You mean like replacing the broken light fixture in the kitchen?"

"Yes, and a few other things."

"Like what?"

Alex blew out a deep breath and lifted his gaze to meet his grandmother's. "Like the peeling paint by the front windows, the worn floor and…the Hobart mixer that broke this morning."

Irene gasped. "The mixer?"

Alex nodded, looking grim.

Annie reached over and covered Irene's hand. "It's all right, Irene. Alex has a call in to the repairman. I'm sure they can fix it."

"I don't know." Irene slowly shook her head. "We bought it refurbished, and it's already been repaired twice."

Alex's eyebrows dipped lower. "How much did the repairs cost?"

"The first time it was around twelve hundred. The second time I think it was two thousand."

Annie swallowed and looked at Alex. She had no idea it cost that much to repair bakery equipment.

"Harry and I tried to find out how much money we have on hand." Alex glanced at the box on the counter. "But we couldn't quite figure out your system."

"I'm afraid it's not much of a system. I just try to pay the bills when they're due." Irene raised a shaky hand to her forehead. "Your grandfather was always better at handling the finances."

"It's okay, Gram. I'll help you."

She looked up. "Really? You'll go over the finances with me?"

"Of course. I'm sure if we put our heads together we can sort things out and make a plan."

She reached over and squeezed his hand. "Thank you. I've been so worried, and I've been praying someone would help me out."

"Well, you don't have to worry anymore." Alex retrieved the box and carried it over to the kitchen table.

Annie peeked over the edge. More than a dozen file folders and piles of envelopes filled the bottom half of the box. She darted a glance at Alex. Straightening out the bakery finances looked as if it would be a daunting task. "Would you like a cup of tea, Irene?"

"Thank you, dear. That sounds lovely."

Annie filled the teapot and set it on the stove while Alex settled in at the table next to his grandmother. He reached in the box and pulled out a few pieces of unopened mail, then patiently waited while his grandmother tore open the first envelope. She read the invoice aloud. He nodded, his expression neutral, but slight lines fanned out around his eyes and creased his forehead.

She'd been wrong about him. He carried just as much responsibility as she did, maybe more. Even if it was challenging and time-consuming, he seemed to want to do what was best for his grandmother. She smiled as she watched him, her heart warming. A man with such a caring heart was a rare find...a rare find indeed.

Chapter Five

Alex grabbed his gym bag from the trunk and trudged up the steps to the back door. He had hoped the workout would clear his head and ease the stress that had been building over the past week. But his mind still felt like a jumbled mess of conflicting thoughts.

The bakery finances were a disaster. He and his grandmother had worked on them for two hours yesterday afternoon and three this morning.

The problem wasn't just poor sales. His grandmother's haphazard bookkeeping made it almost impossible to get a good picture of actual income and expenses. But one thing was clear—there wasn't enough money in the bakery account to pay for the equipment repairs and updates on the building. They barely had enough to cover November salaries for their three employees, let alone take out any money for his grandmother's needs.

As much as he hated to be the one to drop the bomb, he had to level with her. It was time to close Jameson's.

He walked inside and glanced around the empty kitchen. Where was Annie? He was used to seeing her working at the counter or stove, cooking something delicious. That thought made him smile.

Since he had apologized for his reaction to yesterday's burnt breakfast, things had seemed better between them. It was almost as if they had moved back into their comfortable friendship, yet there was something different about it. He supposed that was to be expected after ten years apart. For some reason that bothered him.

The sound of voices in the living room drew him down the hallway. "Hey, Gram, I'm home," he called.

"I'm in here, hon."

He found her watching TV from her recliner with her feet up and a cozy afghan covering her legs. He glanced around but didn't see Annie. He kissed his grandmother's forehead. "You look like you're enjoying yourself."

"I am. I'm watching my cooking show." Her cheery expression lifted his sagging spirits. Surely she'd understand and accept the changes that were coming. She might even be glad to have the burden of running the bakery lifted off her shoulders.

"What are they making today?"

She sent him a mischievous grin. "Pumpkin cheesecake."

He cocked his head. "Well, don't get any ideas. Cheesecake is definitely not on your healthy food list."

"I know, but I can still enjoy watching them make it."

"Doesn't that feel a little like torturing yourself?"

She waved the idea away. "Not at all. Now, go on, put your things away and let me finish my show."

He chuckled and headed up the stairs. A bumping sound overhead made him stop and look up. Then he heard a long swishing noise that sounded like someone sliding a box across the attic floor.

When he reached the upstairs hall, he saw that the folding ladder to the attic had been pulled down. He looked up into the dark opening. "Annie, are you up there?"

"Yeah, I'm looking for a box of Thanksgiving decorations. Irene said they're here, but I can't seem to find them."

He grinned and shook his head. His grandmother hated to throw anything away. "I'll come up and give you a hand."

"Thanks. You might want to bring a flashlight."

"Okay." He dropped his gym bag by his bedroom door, hustled down to the kitchen and took a flashlight from the cabinet under the sink. Then he returned to the second floor and climbed the squeaky folding ladder to the attic.

Cool air fanned across his face, and a dry, dusty scent tickled his nose. He clicked on his flashlight and scanned the dark recesses under the eaves. Several green plastic totes and a long line of old luggage filled the area on the right. On the left, Annie knelt next to a jumbled stack of cardboard boxes. "Wow, I haven't been up here in ages."

"Watch your head." Annie lightly touched her forehead. "I'm speaking from experience."

"Sorry."

"It's just a little bump." She sent him a half smile, then turned back to the boxes. "Irene has all kinds of stuff up here."

"Yes, she's quite a saver." He squatted next to Annie and noted the subtle scent of vanilla floating in the air around her. He leaned closer and pulled in a shallow breath. She smelled just like a sugar cookie with buttercream frosting.

Annie turned. Her gaze connected with his, and her eyes widened. Only a few inches separated them.

Awareness rippled through him, and his heartbeat kicked up a notch. She not only smelled great, she looked very pretty up close.

Her lips parted as though she was going to speak, then she looked down and broke eye contact. "I found a lot of Christmas decorations," she said, her voice slightly higher than usual. "I grouped them over there." She pointed her flashlight beam toward the green totes by the opening in the attic floor.

He watched her carefully in the pale light. Had she sensed the connection, too? Was that what he'd seen in her eyes?

"I've been labeling the boxes as I go," she continued, but her voice sounded normal now. Whatever she'd thought or felt had passed. He was probably just imagining things because of his own reaction.

He pulled in a deep breath and shook off those thoughts. "Labeling the boxes and totes is a good idea. That'll help next time she sends us up here for something."

But then it hit him. He wouldn't be around the next time his grandmother needed something from the attic. Who would help her bring down the Christmas decorations? Would Annie and Emma still be here at Christmas? Where would he celebrate the holiday?

He pushed those questions away and read what Annie had written on the boxes. Pots and Pans. Christmas Ornaments. Vacation Keepsakes. Easter/Spring Decorations. Fishing Gear.

Annie tapped one of the boxes closest to him. "Looks like you stored a few things up here, too."

He gave an embarrassed chuckle. "I forgot about that."

"This one has basketball trophies and your high-school yearbooks. And that one has your snowboard boots and gloves."

"Wow, you found my boots?" He hadn't been snowboarding for seven or eight years, but he couldn't resist the idea of taking a look. He crawled over and opened the box. The boots lay on top of a pile of old shirts and jeans.

He took them out, wishing he could get some time on the slopes this winter, but that wasn't likely once he returned to San Francisco. Setting the boots aside, he grabbed an old shirt and held it up. "Wow, this is ancient." He tossed it back in the box, closed the flaps and shoved the container toward the opening in the attic floor. "I might as well toss this stuff. I'll never wear it."

"Wait. There are other things in there besides clothes."

"Like what?"

"The photo album you made during your senior year for Mrs. Beyer's class…and your Bible and journals."

He stared at her for a second. "They're in this box?"

She nodded. "Sorry. I wasn't trying to snoop."

"No, it's okay." But heat radiated into his neck and face.

"I saw the clothes, and I was going to ask you if we could donate them to charity, but then I looked a little deeper and saw the album and Bible." She waited until he looked her way again. "You should save those, Alex. They're special."

Suddenly the attic felt too small, and he scooted away. "Right. Thanks. I'll take a look later."

Why did he feel so awkward about her discovering he'd left his Bible behind when he went to college? The truth was, he'd not only left his Bible behind, he'd walked away from the faith his parents and grandparents had taught him when he was a boy. He pushed those convicting thoughts away and cleared his throat. "So, no Thanksgiving decorations?"

"Not yet. But I have a few more boxes to check." She crawled over and opened the next one.

Alex followed her. "What's in there?"

"Looks like camping gear."

He clenched his teeth, and a shudder passed through him. Painful memories came rushing back, but he pushed them away. The last thing he wanted to see or think about was anything to do with camping.

She scooted over and opened the next box. "This is it!" She sent him a triumphant smile and pushed it toward the opening.

"You go first," he said. "I'll take the box."

She climbed down, then he tugged the box of decorations over the edge and descended the ladder. When he reached the hallway, he brushed the dust off his hands then closed the attic door, leaving the box with his Bible and journals in the dark.

"Oh, I forgot to mention, I found a few boxes of business records and tax returns for the bakery. Do you think you'll need those?"

"Maybe. I'm not sure." His thoughts returned to his grandmother's failing business, and his spirits deflated.

"What is it, Alex? What's wrong?"

He looked up and met her gaze. "I need your help, Annie."

"What kind of help?"

"We've got to convince Gram it's time to close the bakery."

Her dark eyes flashed. "Alex, you can't do that. It'll break her heart."

"I don't think we have a choice."

"But you know how much it means to her. That's her history, something she and John built together. If you take that away, I'm afraid she'll just give up."

He clenched his jaw.

"You've got to find some way to keep it open."

"Come on, Annie, we have got to face reality. The shop is not making enough to cover expenses. Gram's been using her savings to keep it afloat. She can't keep doing that."

She sagged back against the wall. "I didn't realize things were that bad."

"Well, they are." His voice came out gruffer than he intended.

She sent him a wounded look.

"Maybe I can find a buyer—" he backpedaled "—someone who can invest in the business and update the shop. That would be the best outcome for Gram."

"How would you do that?"

He blew out a deep breath, already doubting the possibility. "I'll talk to other business owners, see what I can learn, but I can't promise anything."

"How much do you think it would cost to update the shop?"

"We're likely talking several thousand dollars."

"Maybe you could get a business loan from the bank."

"Even if we could, Gram has to retire. She can't keep managing Jameson's."

"Well…what if you hired someone else to manage it?"

"How would that help Gram? Paying a new manager would swallow up more income. Besides, who'd want to take over a run-down bakery that's not making a profit?"

She raised her chin and looked him in the eye. "I would."

He blinked. "Are you serious?"

"I hate the idea of closing the bakery, and I have culinary training. Maybe I could make it work."

"Look, I appreciate you wanting to help, but I don't know if Jameson's is worth saving. People want healthy, trendy food now, not deep-fried desserts that are going to clog their arteries and give them a heart attack."

She straightened, looking offended. "Desserts are not evil. And having a doughnut or cupcake once in a while is not going to give someone a heart attack."

"Tell my grandmother that."

"Alex, come on, be reasonable."

He lifted his hands. "I'm being perfectly reasonable. The bakery's books are in the red. Gram can't run the shop anymore. It's time to admit defeat and let it go."

"Why are you so set on closing? Can't you think outside the box just a little?"

Heat flashed into his face. "Hey, I'm trained to think

outside the box. That's what I do every day. But I'm also a realist."

She huffed and rolled her eyes.

"Look, I'm leaving in twelve days. I don't see how I could find someone to buy the business in that short a time, so I don't think we have a choice."

The disappointment in her eyes hit him like a punch in the gut.

"I have to do what's best for my grandmother, and closing Jameson's is the only option that makes sense."

"You really think that's what's best for your grandmother?" Annie shook her head. "The real problem is you're in such a rush to get back to San Francisco, you won't even consider a plan to save the bakery!" She lifted her chin, and her nostrils flared. "I thought you were different—that you actually had a heart in there." She poked him in the chest. "Obviously I was wrong." She spun away, ran down the stairs and slammed her bedroom door.

Alex stared after her, his pulse pounding out a wild beat. Now he'd done it. Couldn't she understand this was a no-win situation? But as her piercing words replayed through his mind, doubts rose. Was she right? Was he more concerned about getting back to work than saving his grandmother's business? And if that was true, what did it say about him? And even more important—what was he going to do about it?

Chapter Six

Annie paced across her room. At any second Alex was going to march through the door and confront her for her outburst.

Oh, why hadn't she just held her tongue instead of blurting out her frustration? It wasn't her job to save the bakery. And even if it was her responsibility, she would never convince Alex to change his mind by insulting him.

Her stomach roiled and twisted.

What if he fired her? Where would they go? She didn't have enough money to rent her own apartment. She'd used her last paycheck to cover their medical bills and car insurance.

They couldn't go back to Lilly's. They'd worn out their welcome there after staying with her for almost a month. And staying with Courtney in her one-bedroom apartment wasn't a good situation. Sharing a hide-a-bed in the living room meant neither she nor Emma got a good night's sleep.

She sank onto the edge of the bed and closed her eyes. *Lord, You know I need this job. We can't move again. Not so soon. I know I shouldn't have said all those things to Alex, but he is so shortsighted and pigheaded and just about the most irritating man I have ever—*

A knock at her door cut into her prayer, and her eyes flew open.

She swallowed, rose from the bed and walked to the door on unsteady legs. She'd apologize and say she was wrong. She had to hold on to this job. With clammy fingers, she clutched the doorknob and slowly pulled it open.

Irene smiled at her. "I just wanted to thank you for finding those Thanksgiving decorations. I'm sorry you had to crawl around the attic. I really need to get organized and throw some things away, but…" Concern filled her eyes. "Why, Annie, you're white as a sheet. Are you ill?"

Annie lifted a trembling hand and tucked her hair behind her ear. "No, I'm fine."

Irene searched her face, and her eyes widened. "What happened to your forehead?"

Annie ran her finger over the tender lump. It felt much larger than when she'd first checked. "Oh, I bumped my head on one of the beams in the attic, but it's nothing, really. I'm okay." She glanced in the mirror over the dresser and pulled in a sharp gasp. The lump looked red and swollen.

Irene pursed her lips. "Bumps on the head can be very serious." She took Annie's arm and guided her to the bed. "Why don't you lie down, and I'll go get a cold pack?"

"Oh, Irene, you don't have to do that."

"No arguing. We've got to get some ice on there before you turn all black-and-blue."

Annie gave in and lay down, all the while feeling a bit ridiculous. But Irene was so insistent, and she didn't want to upset her.

"That's the way." Irene bustled over and took the afghan from the back of the chair, then laid it over Annie.

The blanket felt soft against her skin, and the pillows were plush and comforting.

Irene smiled. "It's about time you let someone take care of you for a change."

"Thanks, but really, I'm fine."

"We'll see about that." She adjusted her glasses and leaned closer to look at Annie's forehead. "My, that does look like a nasty bump. But I'm sure it will calm down as soon as we get some ice on it." She straightened. "You just lie still and rest. I'll be right back."

Annie glanced at the clock. "I have to pick up Emma from school in a few minutes."

"Don't worry. Alex can pick her up."

"No!" Annie sat up. "He doesn't have time for that."

"Nonsense. I'm sure he won't mind." She pointed at Annie. "Now, lie down and stay put."

Annie settled back against the pillows. Great! Now Alex was really going to be put out with her.

She wrestled with those thoughts for a couple minutes while the painful lump on her forehead throbbed. Maybe she should just take a pain reliever and go find Alex, then she could apologize and catch him before Irene sent him off to get Emma.

As she was about to get up, Alex strode into the bedroom carrying an ice pack. His face was set in a stern frown as he leveled his icy-blue gaze at her. "I thought you said it was just a little bump?"

"I'm okay." She swung her legs over the side of the bed and started to sit up.

But he placed his hand on her shoulder and glared at her forehead. "It looks like a goose egg. Lie down."

With an exasperated huff, she flopped back onto the pillows. "Goodness, you're worse than your grandmother."

He settled the cold pack on her forehead. The cool weight sent a shock through her, and she sucked in a quick breath.

"Too cold?"

"Yes…I mean no. It's fine." The frosty pack numbed the pain shooting across her forehead.

He crossed his arms and continued to glare at her.

"I wish you'd stop looking at me like that."

"Like what?"

"Like you're ready to bite my head off."

His expression eased. "Sorry. I'm not mad. I'm just concerned."

"Oh, is that what you call it?" She closed her eyes. She hated feeling at odds with him, but she wasn't about to let him come in here and treat her like a disobedient child. She was a grown woman, and she'd been taking care of herself for several years. She didn't need some overbearing, mean—

"Annie." His gentle, pleading tone broke through her thoughts.

She opened her eyes. His glare was gone, replaced by a softer expression. Her breath caught in her throat, and she had to force out her reply. "What?"

"I was thinking about what you said in the hall, about the bakery."

Regret washed away the last of her anger. "I'm sorry, Alex. I never should've called you heartless. I just—"

He held up his hand. "No, you were right. I'm feeling the pressure to get back to work, and I haven't seriously considered any other options besides closing down. But if you meant what you said about managing the bakery, I'm willing to consider it staying open."

She stared at him. "You're serious?"

"I am if you are." A hopeful light shone in his blue eyes. "We'd have to develop a new business plan and go to the bank for a loan, but if you want to take it on, I'm open to it."

A smile rose from her heart and burst across her face. She lifted her hand and touched the cold pack on her forehead. "Wow, you really are serious."

He grinned and nodded. "Of course, my grandmother will have to agree to whatever plan you suggest, but I think she would be thrilled to see Jameson's stay open."

She smiled up at him, the bump on her forehead forgotten. "Thanks, Alex. I'm sure with us all working together we can find a way to save the bakery."

Alex settled at one end of the couch and propped his feet up on the ottoman. Flaming logs in the fireplace crackled and hissed, spreading warmth and flickering light around the room. The scent of popcorn hung in the air, along with the fragrance of a pumpkin-spice candle burning on the coffee table. He took a sip of coffee and let its soothing warmth settle his thoughts.

His grandmother sat in her recliner with her feet up and a knitting project in her lap. Annie and Emma sat across from him on the love seat, snuggled up together with a book open between them.

A smile crept across his lips as Annie began reading.

"One day a rich young man came to Jesus and asked him, 'Good teacher, what should I do to be sure I have eternal life?' Jesus answered and said, 'Why do you call me good? Only God is good.'"

Emma wrinkled her nose. "Why did he say that?"

"Jesus asked him a question to get him thinking." Annie smiled and tapped Emma's forehead. "Jesus knows we learn more when we think things through and find out the answers for ourselves."

Emma smiled and nodded. She was an intelligent child, but could a five-year-old really understand a concept like that? He supposed if Annie read to her often and they discussed what she read, Emma might be able to catch the meaning. But he had to admit it surprised him.

Annie continued the story. "'Jesus told him to keep these commandments: love your neighbor as yourself, don't murder, always tell the truth, and be sure to honor and obey your parents.'"

"I know a verse about that," Emma said. "'Children, obey your parents in the Lord, for this is right.'"

Irene chuckled. "That's a verse every child should memorize."

Emma sat up straighter. "I learned it for my class at church. And I know a lot more verses. You want to hear 'um?"

Annie patted Emma's knee. "Let's finish the story and see if we have time for that when we're done."

"Okay." She leaned back against her mother.

Annie's expression grew serious. "This rich young man loved his money more than he loved God."

Emma frowned. "That's not good."

"No, it's not. Jesus wants to have first place in our hearts and lives. So He told the young man, 'Go and sell what you own, give to the poor, and you will have treasure in heaven, then come and follow me.'"

"Did he do it?" Emma looked up, her expression full of hope.

"No. The Bible says he went away sad because he was very rich."

Emma's shoulders sagged. "He didn't go with Jesus?"

"No, he didn't," Annie said softly.

"How come?"

Annie thought for a moment. "I suppose he didn't like the idea of giving away his money or leaving home to go with Jesus."

Alex stared at the fire, pondering the story. Was he like

that rich young man? He made a good salary, but he didn't think he loved money. He liked to stick to his own plan, though, and run his own life without much thought of what God wanted him to do. What would Jesus think of that?

"I don't have much money," Emma said, "but I would give it to Jesus if he asked me."

Alex's stomach clenched. Could he say the same thing?

Annie slipped her arm around Emma. "I know you would, sweetie."

Alex set his coffee cup aside, as uneasiness tightened his chest. For the past ten years, he'd focused on building his career, becoming successful and making as much money as possible. He'd stopped attending church, and all thoughts of faith and serving others went on the back burner. Of course, he'd never stopped loving Gram, but his visits home diminished to one or two a year, with only occasional phone calls.

How had his life gotten so off track? When had he drifted into such selfish patterns that were so far from what his parents and grandparents had taught him?

Annie glanced at her watch. "It's time for you to get ready for bed."

Emma stuck out her lower lip. "But I'm not tired."

"It's a school night. You need your rest, so off you go."

Emma slowly rose from the couch, looking more tired than she wanted to admit. She trooped over to Irene and gave her a hug.

Gram smiled, looking delighted as she held the little girl tight. "Good night, Emma. I'll see you in the morning."

Emma turned and looked at Alex with shy, searching eyes.

His heart melted. He sat forward and held out his arms. She hurried across the room, stepped into his embrace and wrapped her arms tightly around his neck.

He closed his eyes, breathing in the scent of marshmallows and hot cocoa. The warmth and trust in her hug caught him by surprise. His throat suddenly felt tight, and he had to force out his words. "Good night, Emma. Sleep tight."

"G'night." She let go and stepped back, her expression warm and her dark brown eyes glowing with affection and trust.

Annie looked down at him with a tender smile. "Come on, Emma." She laid her hand on her daughter's shoulder and guided her out of the room.

Alex sat back, watching them go. Emma was a sweet kid. Annie was doing a great job raising her. The more time he spent with them, the more he sensed a special connection growing between him and Annie.

A warning flashed through him, sending a reminder to be careful. He had a job and life back in San Francisco, and falling for a hometown girl was not part of his plan. Sure, he wanted to get married and have a family someday. But this wasn't a good time to think about getting serious with anyone, especially when things at work were so uncertain. And the last thing he wanted to do was hurt Annie.

Still, he couldn't deny the attraction he felt toward her. He and Annie were friends, and perhaps they would become business partners if she ended up running the bakery for his grandmother.

But that was the only role he intended to let her fill in his life.

Annie grabbed her purse and three plastic grocery bags from the backseat. Emma unbuckled her seat belt and climbed out of the car on the other side.

"Please take your backpack," Annie called before her daughter could make her escape.

Emma sighed, but she turned and slung the backpack over her shoulder.

Annie's heart clenched as she watched her daughter trudge

up the walk toward Irene's front door. More than a week had passed since she and Emma had moved in with Irene and Alex, but her daughter still didn't seem settled. She woke up once or twice every night, calling for Annie. And during the day, she seemed more clingy than usual.

It hadn't been an easy transition for Annie, either. Spending so much time with Alex stirred up her emotions, making her feel awkward around him—although Alex seemed clueless. She'd wondered if he would fire her and send them packing after the blowup yesterday, but he hadn't.

She followed her daughter up the front steps, her thoughts stuck on Alex. What had he been doing all day? Would he really follow through on the idea of remodeling Jameson's and hiring her as manager, or was he out there right now looking for someone else to buy it? Did he think she'd be a good manager? Did he ever think of the possibility of them being more than friends?

Oh, this was silly. She needed to stop thinking about Alex like that. He was her friend and employer. That was it. There was no sense in hoping for anything more.

"Mom, are you coming?" Emma stood by the front door.

Annie hustled across the porch and let them in. Emma dropped her backpack on the floor and headed down the hall.

Annie picked up the backpack. She didn't see Irene, so she tiptoed down the hall and peeked in her bedroom door. Irene lay on the bed, covered with a blue-and-yellow quilt and snoring softly.

Annie returned to the kitchen to unload the groceries and tackle the dirty dishes left from her afternoon cooking spree. Emma walked into the kitchen.

"So how was school today?" Annie rinsed a sticky bowl and set it in the dishwasher.

"Okay." Emma sighed and leaned against the cabinet next to the sink.

Annie studied her daughter. Emma usually came home bursting with stories about her day. The way Emma stared across the room and chewed her lip hinted at a problem.

"Did Mrs. Carlton read more about Squanto and the Pilgrims?"

Emma shook her head and looked down at the floor.

"Did you play with Haley at recess?"

"No."

"Why not? I thought she was your best friend."

Emma shrugged.

Annie grabbed a towel, dried her hands and knelt in front of Emma. "What is it, sweetie? What's wrong?"

Emma's chin wobbled, and tears flooded her eyes. "How come I don't have a daddy?"

Annie stifled a gasp, then reached for her daughter and wrapped her in a tight hug. "Oh, sweetie. You have a daddy. He just doesn't live here with us."

"Why not?" Emma's voice came out in a choked whisper. "Haley's daddy lives with her."

Annie closed her eyes and sent off a silent plea for help. She knew she would have to answer these questions someday, but she thought it would be years away. She gently released her daughter and leaned back so she could see her face. "Why don't we get a snack, and then we can sit down and talk about it, okay?"

Emma sniffed and nodded.

Annie's mind spun as she opened the refrigerator and debated what she would say to her daughter. She couldn't tell her that her father didn't even know she existed. That would be too devastating. She'd just have to ask Emma some questions and see what brought this up.

"I made some applesauce this morning." She reached for two bowls, though she wasn't sure she would be able to eat any. "Shall I sprinkle cinnamon on yours?"

"Okay." Emma walked over to her backpack and unzipped it. "My teacher says I have to give you a paper about our feel trip."

"You mean field trip?" Annie forced a smile.

Emma cocked her head, looking puzzled. "That's what I said."

The new topic eased Annie's fears for the moment. "Where is your class going?"

Emma shrugged and held out the note. "I can't 'member."

Annie scanned the information. "It says you're going to Hoffman's Dairy Farm. You're going to watch them milk the cows and make butter and cheese. You're even going to sample some ice cream." Emma loved ice cream.

But her daughter's somber expression didn't change. She took her bowl of applesauce, murmured thank-you and carried it over to the kitchen table.

Annie sent off another silent prayer and sat next to Emma. "So what made you think to ask about your…daddy?" Even saying the word made her feel off balance.

"Haley said her daddy bought her a new bike for her birthday. And they went for a ride at the park."

"That sounds fun."

"She asked what my daddy got for me." Emma stirred her applesauce. "I said nothing 'cause I don't have a daddy."

Annie's heart twisted. She laid her hand over Emma's. "All children have a mommy and a daddy. That's God's plan for the family. But not all mommies and daddies stay together to raise their children."

Emma looked up at her. "So where's my daddy?"

Annie pressed her lips together. Memories heavy with pain twisted through her, and she had to force out the words. "Your daddy moved away before you were born. I don't know where he lives now. So it's always been just you and me. But a mom and a daughter are still a family."

Emma swirled her spoon through her applesauce. "I wish my daddy lived here."

Annie looked into her daughter's sorrowful eyes. This was a new level of suffering for Emma, and it was Annie's fault.

She reached over and tenderly brushed her daughter's hair back from her forehead. "I understand what you're saying, sweetie. You wish you had a daddy who lived with us and was a part of our family."

Emma nodded, a glimmer of hope reflected in her eyes.

Annie's heart plummeted to a new low. A father...that was what every little girl wanted and needed, but it was the one thing Annie could never give her daughter. No matter how much she wished a godly man would step into that role of husband and father for her and Emma, she had no power to make it happen. Annie's eyes burned as she tried to steel herself against her daughter's disappointment. But it was useless. The painful consequences of her foolish choices had hurt them both, so much more than she could ever have imagined.

Alex heard voices in the kitchen as he crossed the living room. It sounded like Annie and Emma.

"So where's my daddy?" Emma asked.

He stopped and strained to hear Annie's answer. Maybe he shouldn't listen in on their conversation, but that same question had cycled through his mind several times this past week.

"Your daddy moved away before you were born." Annie's voice sounded more tense than usual. "I don't know where he lives now."

He clenched his jaw and scowled. What kind of man would walk away from a pregnant woman and her unborn child? He could've at least stuck around and helped out until Emma was born.

"I wish my daddy lived here."

Emma's soft reply cut him to the heart. Poor kid. All she wanted was a regular family, including a father who loved her.

He could identify. He'd lost his dad when he was twelve, in a flash flood that swept through their campground. His mother and brother had also been pulled in by the raging current and drowned.

Harrowing memories flashed through his mind, but he quickly closed that door, shoving them away into the darkest corner of his heart. What good did it do to think about it now? He could never go back and change anything that had happened. That one terrible night had altered the course of his life forever.

Closing his eyes, he leaned against the wall and pulled in a deep breath, trying to steady his surging emotions.

Annie's voice cut through the silence. "I understand what you're saying, sweetie. You wish you had a daddy who lived with us and was a part of our family." The sorrow in Annie's voice hit him hard.

Someone tapped him on the shoulder, and he nearly jumped out of his skin.

His grandmother's lips parted as though she was going to speak. But he lifted his finger in front of his mouth and guided her away from the kitchen and down the hallway.

"What's going on?" Irene whispered.

"Come on," he said, keeping his voice low. He led her into her bedroom and shut the door.

"Why are we sneaking around?"

"I don't want Annie to know we heard what she said to Emma."

"But I didn't hear anything," Irene said, looking disappointed. "What did I miss?"

"Emma was asking about her father."

"Oh." Irene's eyes grew round. "What did Annie say?"

He related the few things he'd heard, the weight of it clamping down on his heart again. "Has she said anything else to you about Emma's father?"

"No, she told me about Emma in a Christmas card the year she was born, but she didn't say anything about the father." She frowned and crossed her arms. "Terrible man, deserting them like that."

"I'm sure there's more to the story."

Irene pulled back. "You're not defending him, are you?"

"No. It just makes me wonder what happened." Alex shoved his hands into his pants pockets. "I don't understand it. What guy in his right mind would walk away from someone as great as Annie?"

Her eyes widened, and a slow smile spread across her lips.

Heat flashed up his neck. "I mean she's got a lot of good qualities. It just doesn't make sense."

"You're right," Gram said, her eyes glowing. "She's a kind and caring person, an excellent mother, and I'm sure she'll make someone a wonderful wife."

His face burned, and he gave Gram a quick nod. "I'm sure she will." Then he turned and strode away before she could say anything else.

Of course he wanted Annie to be happy and get married someday. That was a given. But as he considered what that would actually mean, his chest tightened. Would Emma's father come back into the picture, or would Annie meet someone else? The painful pressure in his chest increased. He blew out a deep breath and tried to shake off the crazy feeling. He had enough on his plate without worrying about some guy swooping in and snatching Annie away.

Chapter Seven

Annie carried her computer over to the dining-room table and sat down with Irene. "Here, take a look at this website." She turned the computer so her friend could see.

Irene adjusted her glasses and studied the home page of The Corner Café in Rockwood. "Oh, my, that's lovely." She peered at the screen for a few more seconds. "It's stylish and modern, but it still looks comfortable and homey. I like it!"

Annie nodded. "Their history is a lot like Jameson's. They evolved from a traditional, family-owned bakery to a contemporary café that's become a hub for the community."

"What kind of changes did they make?"

"They responded to their customer's requests to add more choices to the menu. Look at this." She clicked to the next web page. "They still offer all their original breads and sweets, but now they also serve breakfast and lunch sandwiches, soups, salads, panini and pasta."

"That sounds wonderful. Do you think we could offer something similar?"

Annie thought through the preparation needed for that type of menu. "We'd probably have to add some equipment in the kitchen, but not too much more."

Irene nodded, her expression growing more hopeful by

the minute. "But it will take more than updating the kitchen to make us look like this." She pointed to the photo on the screen. "I've got some savings put away. Maybe that would be enough to cover the equipment and furnishings we need."

Annie's train of thought lost steam at the mention of Irene's savings. Draining her friend's bank account was a risky prospect. What if these changes weren't enough to save Jameson's? What would happen to Irene then? Maybe she shouldn't get Irene's hopes up until she ran these ideas by Alex. But surely he'd see that remodeling Jameson's was the only way to bring in new customers and make it profitable again.

Annie laid her hand on Irene's shoulder. "I think this is just what we need, but let's talk to Alex and see what he says."

"Good idea. That boy has a head for business."

Hearing Irene refer to Alex as a boy made her smile. But it made sense. Irene had raised Alex since he'd lost his parents and brother when he was twelve. Irene rarely spoke about the tragedy, but Annie remembered hearing others say they'd been caught in a flash flood while they were on vacation. Alex had been the only survivor.

Annie shivered. Alex never talked about his parents or brother. Maybe their loss was still too painful, or maybe he had just moved on—but the first scenario seemed more likely.

"Yes, let's show Alex. I'm sure he'll know what to do next. The bakery finances were a tangled mess until he helped me sort everything out." Irene sighed and shook her head. "I had no idea our income had dipped so low. My dear John would be so disappointed in me if he could see what's happened."

"Oh, no, Irene, I'm sure he'd understand. And now that you've got a clear picture of the situation, you can make new plans and look ahead to a brighter future."

"Yes, the future…that has to be our focus now." Irene studied the screen once more.

Annie's gaze shifted, and in her mind's eye she saw Jameson's freshly painted in warm, inviting colors, with new, comfortable seating and cheerful decor. Customers would fill the café and enjoy the delicious new menu items she would create. "I think our neighbors and friends will like our fresh, healthy food."

"Of course they will. People have always loved Jameson's, and now it will be even better."

"We'll make a special effort to keep your current customers," Annie continued. "And we'll welcome a whole new circle of friends to Jameson's."

"I love it!" Irene's smile lit up her face. "It sounds like a perfect fit for Fairhaven."

The back door opened. Annie and Irene glanced toward the kitchen.

"Gram, I'm home." Alex walked into the dining room. Irene and Annie exchanged smiles.

He searched their faces. "What are you ladies up to?"

"Annie and I have been surfing the web, looking for ways to update the bakery, and I think we've found just what we want."

He cocked his head. "Really?"

"Yes, come take a look." Irene motioned him over.

Alex joined them at the table, and Annie explained her ideas. When she finished, she clasped her hands in her lap and waited for his reply.

He tapped his fingers on the table and studied the computer screen. "You're talking about making some expensive changes. I'm not sure we should take on a big project like that."

"Nonsense!" Irene pushed back from the table. "This is

just what we need to save Jameson's and bring in a new generation of customers."

He rubbed his jaw, still looking doubtful. "I'm not sure, Gram. Doing this much work on the building would mean closing the bakery for several months, and that would put your employees out of work."

Annie straightened. "Why not keep those employees on and have them help with the renovations?"

"Good idea!" Gram said. "We could do the work in phases. Things like painting the exterior, putting up a new awning and adding planters wouldn't take too long. Then we could do the interior work."

Alex leaned back, his forehead creased with a slight frown. "This is going to cost a lot. Are you sure you want to make this kind of investment?"

"It's either that or close down, and I definitely want to keep the bakery open."

Annie's stomach tightened. "It's a risk, Irene. If things don't go as we hoped, you could lose your savings."

Irene waved away her concern. "I'm sure it'll be a huge success. And there's no other way I'd rather see my money spent."

"Wait a minute." Alex shifted his serious gaze to Annie. "What do you mean lose her savings?"

"Irene said she'd rather borrow from her savings than get a business loan from the bank."

Alex rubbed the back of his neck. "But that's your retirement money, Gram."

"I don't see any other way to get this done quickly."

"I'm not sure that's wise. Let me talk to a few people."

"Who?"

"An accountant, a lawyer, a banker, maybe someone from the Small Business Administration."

Annie shifted in her chair. "I already looked online at

SBA's website for information on applying for a business loan. The process is pretty daunting. You have to write up a complete business plan and gather a lot of financial information. Borrowing from Irene's savings would be a lot quicker. We might have to close for only a few weeks, as opposed to months, if we finance the changes ourselves."

Alex narrowed his eyes. "Maybe those steps recommended by the SBA are there to protect business owners and keep them from making a foolish mistake."

Heat flooded Annie's cheeks. "Remodeling Jameson's is not a foolish mistake."

His eyebrows dipped. "That's not what I said."

"But that's what you're implying."

"No, I'm just trying to get you to slow down and think realistically. We have to be sure we can make a profit and pay back the money you'd take from my grandmother's savings."

"I know it's a risk," Annie said, "and it will take a lot of work, but it's a worthy project with great potential."

Irene looked up at him. "Your grandfather and I spent decades building our business. We have a good reputation and loyal customers, and I think updating Jameson's is the next step to making it profitable again."

Alex looked back and forth between Annie and Irene. "All right. I can see you've both got your hearts set on this. But I'd still like to see a business plan and show it to a few people. If the facts line up and they agree, then I'll feel better about moving ahead." His steady gaze rested on Annie. "That's the only way I'm willing to risk my grandmother's savings."

Annie nodded. "I understand, and I'm sure we can come up with a plan you'll like."

Irene stood and linked arms with Annie and Alex. "So we're agreed. Annie will draw up the business plan. Alex will show that to some people and get their input, then we'll move ahead and give Jameson's a new lease on life."

Annie nodded and held tightly to Irene's arm. This was a good plan. She felt certain of it. Her gaze shifted to Alex, hoping they'd convinced him they were right. But the shadow of doubt still clouded his eyes. It would take more than positive thinking and a hopeful plan to win him over. She'd have to create a strong business plan that answered all his questions if she was going to ease his fears. And that was exactly what she intended to do.

Alex towed the blue plastic tarp full of fallen leaves out to the street and dumped the load on the growing pile. The trees weren't finished shedding all their leaves yet, but he'd hoped coming outside and doing something physical would clear his mind and ease the tightness in his neck and shoulders.

So far it hadn't helped much. No matter how diligently he raked, one question kept cycling through his mind. Why had he been so hard on Annie about her remodeling ideas?

Sure, he was concerned about his grandmother and feeling pressured to make a decision about the bakery. But her ideas weren't unreasonable. It was just the thought of risking his grandmother's savings that brought out the bear in him.

Should they take a risk like that? What if her plans flopped? He'd be the one footing the bill to care for his grandmother if she lost her investment.

Would that be so terrible? He made a good salary. He could afford to take care of his grandmother if it came to that. But what if he lost his job? He hadn't mentioned that possibility to Annie or his grandmother. They had enough on their minds, and he didn't want to add to their worries.

Maybe it was time he had a little faith…in Annie, and someone else, too. He glanced up at the sky as he strode across the yard and picked up his rake. *God, if You're up there and You're listening, could You give me some help here?*

He gripped the rake as the irony of that plea washed over him. Faith in God and talking to Him in prayer hadn't been a regular part of his life since he lost his parents and brother sixteen years ago.

At first the hurt and anger had been so overwhelming that he couldn't focus his thoughts. Then the angry words came in torrents, but he'd stuffed them down deep inside, nursing a grudge against God for taking his family. In time, all he felt was cold distance that squelched any small flicker of faith left in his heart.

But as he watched Annie pray with Emma and read those Bible stories each night, something had begun to stir in his heart. He didn't know why his parents and brother had been taken. He probably never would. But spending time with Annie eased the ache in his heart. And those embers of faith he thought were dead were beginning to glow and flicker back to life…all because of Annie.

He raked another pile of leaves to the center of the lawn, musing over the way she'd had such a big impact on him in such a short time.

His cell phone buzzed in his pocket. He pulled it out and read Annie's name on the screen. His heart pumped an extra beat as he lifted it to his ear.

"Hey, Alex. I hate to bother you, but I'm stuck—" The sound of a truck roaring by cut off her words.

His heart lurched. "Where are you?"

"I'm on the Five Freeway, just north of Lakeway Drive. I've got a flat tire."

He tensed. "Are you pulled over in a safe spot?"

"Yes, but I can't get one of the lug nuts off." More traffic buzzed past in the background.

"You're trying to change the tire yourself?"

"I've done it once before, but this time—"

"Annie, please get back in the car and lock your doors. I'll come help you."

A second passed before she answered. "Okay, thanks."

"Sit tight. I'll be there in less than ten minutes."

"I'll be watching for you."

He tossed the rake aside and dashed for his car. She was trying to change a tire on the freeway by herself? She hated to bother him? Was that how she felt, as if she was a bother? He growled under his breath as he climbed in and slammed his car door.

Annie stared at the phone in her hand. An eighteen-wheeler barreled by, sending a cold gust of wind swirling around her. She slipped inside her car.

Why did Alex sound so upset? Had she interrupted him while he was doing something important, or was he actually worried about her? The way he'd told her to get in the car and lock the doors sounded more like concern than irritation.

A smile crept across her lips, and a little shiver traveled up her arms. It had been a long time since a man cared enough to worry about her or promise to come and help when she was in trouble.

It had been even longer since she'd dared to ask.

She started the engine, turned on the heat and rubbed her hands together, hoping that would drive away the chill. Glancing in the rearview mirror, she caught a glimpse of her wind-tossed hair and pale face.

She looked as if she'd been hiking through a storm. With a disgusted huff, she reached for her purse, pulled out her lipstick and swiped color across her lips, then tried to smooth down her curls.

Her hand stilled and she stared in the mirror. What was she doing? Alex saw her every day and knew exactly how she looked. He'd seen her in all her frazzled glory, first thing in the morning when she saw her daughter off to school and last thing at night as she tucked Emma into bed.

He would not be impressed by a little lipstick.

Her shoulders sagged and she leaned back. If only Alex would truly see her and care about her the way she cared about him. She tried to squelch that longing, but as she replayed his response to her phone call, the longing grew stronger.

Would he ever see her as more than his old friend and his grandmother's companion?

Closing her eyes, she reigned in her thoughts and turned them into a prayer. *Lord, You know how I feel about Alex. He has so many great qualities I admire. He'd make a wonderful husband and father, but if You don't want me to get involved with him, please help me do something about these feelings. I definitely don't need more complications and heartache. I'd never recover from another broken heart, so if Alex is not the right man for me, please make it so obvious I can't miss it.*

Flashing lights broke through her prayer, and her eyes flew open. A Bellingham police cruiser rolled to a stop behind her car, the red and blue lights pulsing out a warning.

The fading, late-afternoon light made it difficult to see the officer's face, but his silhouette showed a man with broad shoulders wearing a uniform hat.

She hadn't done anything wrong, but her stomach quivered and she clutched the steering wheel tighter. At least two minutes passed before the officer climbed out of his cruiser and walked up to her car.

She rolled down her window, looked up at him and forced a small smile.

He stood at least six feet tall and wore a perfectly pressed black uniform complete with a silver badge and a thick black belt with a holster and gun. He looked down at her with a serious expression. "Afternoon, miss. May I see your license, registration and insurance card?"

"Oh. Sure." She reached for her purse and took out her ID with trembling hands. Maybe she *had* done something wrong. She quickly searched through the glove compartment for the other papers. "I've got a flat tire. That's why I'm stopped here." She handed him her license, registration and insurance card.

He nodded and scanned the items, then narrowed his eyes at her license.

"I've got a spare tire and a jack, but one of the lug nuts is stuck, and I couldn't get the tire off."

His dark eyebrows bunched as he shifted his gaze to the front-left tire. "You tried to change it yourself?"

"Yes." What was it with men? Didn't they think a woman could change a tire? It wasn't that complicated. It just took more strength than she could muster at the moment.

"Do you have Triple A?"

"No, but help is on the way." She held up her cell phone and smiled. "I just made the call."

His gaze connected with hers, and a slight smile tipped his lips. "Good. Looks like you're in a pretty safe place, but I'll wait with you until your friend arrives. Or is it your husband?"

"I'm not married."

His smile warmed a few more degrees. "Hmm, I'm surprised."

Was he actually flirting with her? Her face warmed, and she looked down and bit her lip.

He cleared his throat and struck a more serious pose. "What's in those containers?" He nodded toward the back of her car where she'd set her three totes on the pavement.

"Those are my cooking supplies. I'm a personal chef, and I cook at my clients' homes, so I have to take my tools with me. Keeping them in my trunk makes a lot more sense than toting them in and out of the house each time I need them, and I had to get out the spare tire, so I thought it would be all right to set those—"

He held up his hand to stop her rambling. "It's not a problem. I was just curious." His smile returned. "My name's Marcus Fletcher."

She swallowed. "It's nice to meet you, Marcus. I'm Annie Romano, but I guess you already knew that."

He glanced at her ID once more. "This license is from Oregon. Do you still live in Portland?"

"No, I moved back to Fairhaven recently." She had no idea how long she had to get a Washington license. "I hope that's not a problem."

"No, it's fine. Just be sure to apply for a Washington license before this one expires. That way you can avoid taking the written test."

"Okay, thanks. I'll take care of it."

His appreciative gaze remained on her, and he looked as though he was about to say more, but Alex's car pulled up and parked in front of hers.

"Is that your…friend?" Marcus tipped his head toward the burgundy Camry.

"Yes. That's Alex Jameson. His grandmother owns Jameson's bakery. Do you know him?"

"Nope."

Alex climbed out and strode toward them, a worried frown creasing his forehead. He glanced at her, then nodded to Marcus. "Officer."

Marcus returned the nod, his expression all business. "You're here to help Miss Romano?"

"Yes." He shifted his gaze to Annie and leaned toward the window. "Are you all right?"

Her heart did a funny little skip. "I'm fine."

He straightened and turned to Marcus. "Thanks for stopping, Officer. I'll take it from here."

The two men locked gazes for a couple seconds.

Marcus raised his chin. "I'll wait and be sure she gets back on the road."

"It's not a problem. I've changed plenty of tires."

Marcus looked him over with a doubtful glance.

Annie hopped out of the car and stood between them. "Thanks, Marcus. I appreciate you stopping and waiting with me." She turned to Alex. "The jack and tools are in the trunk." She motioned toward the back of the car, then walked with him. "Thanks for coming. I hope I didn't take you away from something important."

"No. I was just raking leaves."

"I tried it, but I couldn't quite get the leverage I needed to get the lug nuts off."

"I'm glad you called. I don't like the idea of you out here on the freeway down on your hands and knees, changing a tire." He took the jack and wrench from the trunk. "Here, hold these while I grab the spare."

She took the tools and stepped back as he lifted the tire from the trunk, then she followed him around front.

Marcus stood by, his arms crossed as Alex knelt, loosened the lug nuts and removed the flat tire. "Let me know if you need a hand," Marcus added with a slight smile and quick look at Annie.

"No, I've got it." Alex gave a little grunt as he lifted the spare tire into place on the wheel studs.

She pressed her lips together to keep her grin inside. Marcus had obviously picked up on Alex's protective, take-charge attitude.

"I'll roll this to the trunk for you." Marcus pushed the flat tire away before Annie or Alex could object.

Within five minutes, Alex had the lug nuts tightened on

the spare. He lowered the jack and replaced the hubcap, then stood and brushed off his hands. "Okay, Annie, you're all set."

"Thanks. You made that look easy." She sent Alex a warm smile, then turned to Marcus. "Thanks again, Marcus. It's nice to know someone is keeping an eye out for stranded drivers."

He touched the brim of his hat. "Anytime. Glad to help." He glanced at Alex and back at her. "You take care now."

"We will." Alex lifted his hand in a gesture that looked more like *I've got everything under control* than a wave.

Marcus gave his head a slight shake and chuckled as he walked back to his police cruiser.

Alex's brows bunched together. "What's he laughing at?"

Annie shrugged. "Maybe he just thought it was nice the way you took care of everything for me."

Alex huffed. "Yeah, well, I didn't see him getting down on his knees to do any of the real work."

She couldn't hold back her grin this time.

Alex's eyes widened. "What?"

"Nothing."

He looked at the police cruiser and back at her. "So, is he a friend of yours?"

"No, I just met him."

"Then how come you're calling him Marcus?"

She blinked a couple times. "Oh, well, he introduced himself, and I just thought—"

"Annie, come on. That's not smart."

"What do you mean?"

"You shouldn't be so friendly with a guy you just met."

"He's a policeman, Alex, not a criminal."

"Just because he's a policeman doesn't mean you should throw caution to the wind." Alex sounded more irritated than concerned.

She glanced at Marcus seated in his police cruiser. "He seemed nice enough to me."

"Maybe he is, maybe he's not, but I don't think any guy should be looking at you like that."

"For goodness' sake, Alex, you sound like an overprotective big brother."

"Well, I don't want him or anybody else taking advantage of you."

"No one is taking advantage of me."

"Are you going to see him again?"

She stared at Alex. "Not unless he pulls me over and gives me a ticket."

Alex stuffed his hands in his pockets and rocked back on his heels. "Look, I'm sorry. Maybe it's none of my business, but I'm just trying to watch out for you."

"And why would that be your job?"

"Because we're friends." He ground out the statement as though it was painful to him.

She turned away, folded her arms protectively across her stomach and watched Marcus pull back onto the road. He nodded and sent her a smile as he passed. She lifted her hand and waved—but the only guy she cared about was Alex, and he seemed put out with her.

Chapter Eight

Alex followed Annie up the front steps and into the house. His empty stomach rumbled. He hadn't eaten in a while, and he felt hungry and out of sorts.

It was nearly dinnertime, but Annie's flat tire had delayed things, so they wouldn't be eating for a while. Maybe he'd grab a snack, retreat to his room and check email while Annie cooked dinner. At least up there he could have some peace and quiet and not have to deal with anything.

She glanced over at him as she quietly slipped off her jacket, but he looked away and pretended not to notice. He didn't feel like talking to her. Not now.

All the way home he'd replayed Annie's interaction with *Officer* Marcus. He grimaced and gave his head a slight shake, but he couldn't shake off the truth. He didn't like another guy looking at Annie as if she was his favorite dessert. That was the real reason he felt cross, and that irked him even more.

What was the big deal? He was not dating Annie. He had no claim on her. He stuffed his coat in the closet and shut the door harder than necessary.

Annie took a step back and sent him a questioning look.

"Mom, look what I made!" Emma ran toward them

through the living room, wearing an Indian headdress that looked as if it had been cut from a brown grocery sack. The paper feathers flapped in the breeze as she waved her hands and danced around with a broad grin wreathing her face.

"Wow, look at you." Annie knelt and gave Emma a hug.

"It's for Thanksgiving," Emma said, wiggling out of her mother's arms.

"That's very special. Where did you get that idea?"

"Irene and Marian showed me." She pointed toward the kitchen.

"I see. Well, that was certainly nice of them."

"I'm making one for you." She took her mother's hand. "And one for Alex." She held out her other hand to him. "Come and see."

His annoyance faded as he grasped Emma's warm, pudgy fingers and let her pull him toward the kitchen. Annie sent him a tentative smile, and the last of his irritation melted away.

Gram and her friend Marian Chandler, owner of Bayside Books, sat at the kitchen table with coffee mugs in their hands. The scattered remains of several paper grocery bags littered the table, along with Emma's collection of brightly colored felt-tip markers and a pair of child's scissors.

"Welcome home," Gram said with a warm smile.

Annie rested her hand on her daughter's shoulder. "I'm sorry I was gone so long. Thanks for watching Emma."

"Don't worry. We had a delightful time, didn't we, sweetie?"

Emma smiled and bobbed her head. "We had cocoa and popcorn, and then we made Indian hats."

Marian chuckled. "I think it's called a headdress."

"I know." Emma popped the lid off a purple marker and started vigorously coloring another paper feather. "I just forgot for a minute."

Gram and Marian exchanged smiles, obviously enjoying Emma's response.

"So." Irene shifted her gaze from Alex to Annie. "Alex came to your rescue and took care of the flat tire?" The slight smile and gleam in his grandmother's eyes sent a subtle warning through Alex.

"Yes." Annie's cheeks turned a soft pink. She opened the refrigerator and looked inside. "Now I just need to figure out what to do about the tire."

Marian set her mug on the table. "Why don't you go see Brad Fulsome over at T&S Tires? He repaired a tire for me a few months ago, but they also sell new tires if you need one."

"Good idea," Gram added, her face brightening. "Maybe Alex could go with you tomorrow morning. He knows all about things like that."

Annie's eyes flashed. "Oh, no, that's okay. He already helped me enough today. I'm sure I can figure it out." She nodded to Marina. "I'll go to T&S tomorrow and be sure to ask for...what was his name?"

"Brad Fulsome," Marian said. "He's such a nice young man."

An image of single, muscular, thirtysomething Brad Fulsome flashed through Alex's mind, and he quickly shook his head. "I don't mind going with you."

Annie looked at him with wide eyes. "If you're sure you have time."

"It's not a problem." He stepped past Annie and took a bottle of water from the refrigerator. As he closed the door, his arm brushed Annie's, and heat spread through him.

Their gazes connected for a split second, then he shook it off and looked away.

Marian and Irene exchanged secretive smiles. Alex pretended not to notice and strode out of the kitchen.

As he reached the stairs, he realized he'd completely forgotten to get a snack. He huffed out a disgusted breath and kept climbing. It served him right.

Annie hovered over her laptop reviewing the business plan she had been working on for the bakery. There were just a few more sections she needed to fill in, but she'd have to ask Alex for some financial information before she could finish those. That thought made her stomach do a funny little dance, but she quickly squelched her reaction.

This was business. If she and Alex were going to work together on this project, she needed to keep her feelings under control. That was growing harder every day, but she'd just have to deal with it.

She scrolled down the page, checking her work and making a few changes. She reached for her cup of tea, took a sip and was surprised to find it was cold. A quick glance at the clock told her it was twelve-fifteen.

How did it get to be that late? She'd be exhausted tomorrow if she didn't put her computer away and head to bed soon. Maybe she'd just look over the menu section one more time before she called it a night.

"Annie?"

Her heart jumped, and her hand flew to her throat.

"Sorry. I didn't mean to scare you." Alex padded across the kitchen wearing gray sweatpants and a navy T-shirt. His usually neat brown hair was rumpled and messy, making him look more attractive than ever.

She doused that thought and wrapped her arms around herself. "I didn't think anyone was still up."

"I was just reading, and I thought I heard something down here. What are you doing up so late?"

"I'm working on the business plan."

He took a glass from the cabinet. "How's it coming?"

"Okay." She debated the wisdom of sharing the plan with him now or waiting until tomorrow.

"We've only got a few more days before the Thanksgiving holiday."

She nodded, and her heart constricted. Alex would be leaving for San Francisco in nine days. But she didn't want to mention that. Somehow not saying it aloud made it seem less threatening.

"So can I take a look?"

"I'm not done yet."

"I don't mind."

She hesitated a second more. "All right. But I haven't filled in some of the sections yet. It still needs a lot of work."

"I understand it's a work in progress."

She sat back. Would he like what she'd done, or would he think her ideas were silly and not worth the investment?

He placed his hand on the kitchen table next to her and leaned over her shoulder, close enough that she could feel his warm breath on her cheek. The scent of evergreens and spice teased her nose. She pulled in a slow, deep breath and swallowed. Oh, my. That made it worse.

He reached for the track pad and scrolled down the document, his gaze intense as he scanned the photos and read what she'd written.

She closed her eyes and tried to steady her breathing. He obviously had no idea what being this close to him did to her.

"This is good."

Her eyes flew open, and she blinked up at him.

"Very good." His smile spread wider, and charming dimples creased both his cheeks.

A wave of pleasure flowed through her. "You really like it?"

He nodded. "Where'd you learn to put together a business proposal like this?"

"I did one as part of my final project at culinary school. They wanted us to understand the business side of things as well as cooking."

"Sounds like a good program."

"It was." At this close range, she couldn't help noticing the fine lines that fanned out from the corners of his sky-blue eyes, and the dark stubble on his square chin.

He stilled and gazed down at her, seeming to take in each of her features, his warm expression unchanging.

Her heartbeat changed to a rapid flutter, and her mouth suddenly felt as dry as a cotton puff.

What did he see when he looked at her? The tired lines that crossed her forehead, the dark circles under her eyes, the grief she still carried for the choices she'd made? Her heart sank, and she looked away. "It's late. I should get to bed."

He leaned back, his gaze still focused on her. "Yeah." He cleared his throat. "I guess so."

She closed her laptop and stood. As she stepped away from the table, he reached out and touched her arm. She stilled as the warmth of his hand spread up her arm.

"Annie." His voice was soft and low.

She swallowed and slowly raised her gaze to meet his. "Yes?"

"Thanks for everything you're doing. It means a lot."

"I'm glad I can help." She stepped away, and his hand slipped off her arm.

"Good night."

She hurried from the kitchen, clutching her laptop to her chest. Thank goodness he was going to be here only a few more days, because no matter how many times she told herself she did not love Alex Jameson, her heart was not listening.

Annie pushed her full grocery cart around the corner to the next aisle, searching the shelves for canned pumpkin.

She scanned past chopped walnuts, sliced almonds, chocolate chips and coconut, but she didn't see pumpkin anywhere.

Had she missed it in the holiday baking display in the center of the grocery store? Maybe Alex would know where to find it. She chuckled softly and shook her head. Probably not, though he was making a good effort to help her on this shopping trip.

She and Irene had planned the Thanksgiving menu and made the shopping list, but Alex had insisted on coming with her to the store, saying he wanted to be sure they got everything they needed for their special holiday meal.

They'd found all the items on their list except the last two. Alex was now off searching for the sparkling apple cider while she hunted down the canned pumpkin.

Annie looked across the aisle and finally spotted it on the bottom shelf next to the cherry pie filling. She grabbed two cans and added them to her cart.

The thought of baking pumpkin muffins made her smile. They were one of Emma's favorite snacks. It was a light and healthy recipe that Irene would also be able to enjoy without guilt. And she couldn't wait for Alex to try her pumpkin fluff. Her friend Terry from her church in Portland had made it last Thanksgiving. When Annie had asked her for the recipe, Terry had laughed and said it was simply canned pumpkin, light whipped topping and sugar-free vanilla pudding mix. She was sure he'd like it, especially when she served it with gingersnaps.

"Annie?"

She turned and saw her old friend Brianna Lundberg pushing a grocery cart toward her. They had both grown up in Fairhaven and attended the University of Oregon together—at least those first two years until Annie dropped out because she was pregnant with Emma.

Annie greeted her and they exchanged a brief hug. "What brings you back to Fairhaven?" she asked Brianna.

"I'm here visiting my parents for Thanksgiving. How about you?"

"I moved back a few months ago. I've started my own business as a personal chef."

"Wow, that's great." Brianna smiled. "That sounds like something you'd enjoy. I remember you used to love planning the menus for our house parties." She gave Annie's arm a little pat. "And those Tri Delta guys always raved about everything you made."

A shudder traveled through Annie. House parties, especially those with Tri Delta fraternity, were not happy memories. She'd never enjoyed that part of sorority life. She'd pledged looking for friendship and a sense of belonging, and though she'd made a few friends in her sorority, none of them stayed close after she became pregnant. The choices and compromises she'd made to fit in had cost her so much more than she'd ever dreamed.

Brianna took a step closer. "Speaking of Tri Delta…did you hear what happened to Kevin Seagraves?"

Annie pulled in a sharp breath and shook her head.

"I remember you two were friends." Brianna narrowed her eyes. "Didn't you date him for a while?"

Annie's mind spun, and her thoughts flashed back to her second year at college. Spring semester Kevin had swept her off her feet then left her with a broken heart before she had the courage to tell him she was pregnant.

"We only dated for a few months," she finally managed to say.

"Well, it's a good thing you broke it off."

She hadn't. Kevin had been the one to tell her it was over. Then he transferred to Oregon State, leaving her behind—

just like her father had when she was seven, and just like Alex had when she was fifteen.

Annie blinked and forced out her words. "Why? What do you mean?"

"Kevin was arrested for embezzling funds from the company where he worked."

Annie's mouth dropped open.

"I can't believe it, either." Brianna shook her head, looking disgusted. "He has a wife and baby boy. What's going to happen to them now?"

Annie gripped the handle of the shopping cart and tried to stop the dizzy spinning in her head. Kevin was married and had a son? He'd been arrested for embezzlement? It was too much to take in.

"Annie?" Brianna reached out and touched her arm. "Are you all right?"

"Yes, I'm okay. It's just…so terrible. I had no idea. I mean, I knew Kevin had issues, but I never thought he'd do anything illegal like that."

"I know. It's hard to believe, but I saw Paul Sherman and he mentioned it. So I looked online and read the article. The trial is still going on. They said he could get up to thirty years if he's found guilty."

Annie stared at her friend, trying to figure out what to say.

Alex strolled down the aisle toward them, carrying three bottles of sparkling cider. As he drew closer, his carefree expression faded. "Everything okay?"

Panic rose and swirled through Annie. She couldn't tell him about Emma's father. Not here, not now. "Alex, do you remember Brianna Lundberg? She was in my class at Sehome." She forced lightness into her voice, but it still sounded strained.

He glanced at Brianna and shook his head. "Sorry, it's been a while. And I'm not great at remembering names."

Brianna flashed a bright smile and held out her hand. "Well, I remember you." They shook hands. "You played basketball for Sehome, didn't you?"

"That's right." He stepped back and crossed his arms.

She flipped her long blond hair behind her shoulder as her gaze traveled over him. "You look like you're in great shape. Do you still play?"

Annie's eyes widened. She glanced at Alex, checking his reaction.

The small crease between his eyebrows deepened. "A little."

"Great. I'd love to see you play." Brianna sent Alex another teasing smile, then shifted her gaze to Annie. "So are you two…together?"

Annie stifled a gasp and shot a quick look at Alex. He placed the cider in the cart, apparently leaving it up to her to answer the question.

Annie's face flamed. Brianna had a lot of nerve putting her on the spot like that. "I've been taking care of Alex's grandmother since she had a heart attack a few weeks ago." That didn't really answer the question, but it was all Annie intended to say.

"Oh." Brianna waited, looking as though she hoped for more. "Well, I'm sorry to hear about your grandmother. Does she still have that little bakery…what's it called?" She tapped her chin, then smiled. "Oh, yes, Jameson's, isn't it? I should've remembered since that's your last name." She laughed as though that was the funniest joke in the world.

Alex shot Annie a perturbed glance.

"Maybe we can get together this week." Brianna looked at Annie first, then her gaze slid to Alex with a slight lift of her eyebrows. She reached in her purse and pulled out two business cards. She handed one to Annie and the other to Alex. "That's my cell number. Give me a call anytime."

"Thanks." Annie forced out the word then glanced at the card. Willmont Realty, Salem, Oregon. She slipped it into her purse.

Alex stuffed the card in his pants pocket. "We've got to go. I don't want to leave my grandmother alone too long." He placed his hand on Annie's lower back and gave her a gentle push forward.

"Give your grandmother my best. Take care, Annie. Nice to see you again, Alex. Give me a call. I'd love to get together anytime you're free. Things are really boring at my mom and stepdad's..."

Brianna's voice faded as they rounded the corner. Alex dropped his hand, and Annie found herself missing his touch.

"Is she a close friend?"

"Not really. I haven't seen her since I left Eugene."

"Good." He huffed and shook his head.

Annie grinned. "She was always a little over-the-top in the flirting department."

"You can say that again."

A chuckle rose from Annie's throat.

"What is so funny?"

"Nothing. It's just that she really seemed to enjoy seeing you again."

"Well, the feeling was not mutual." He grimaced. Took her business card from his pocket and tore it in half. "Women like that make me want to head for the hills."

He took over pushing the cart and steered them into the shortest checkout line as Annie's heart did a happy little dance. She could hardly keep her smile in check.

Chapter Nine

A crisp fall breeze sent golden leaves tumbling across the driveway as Alex pulled in and parked. He popped the trunk and hopped out of the car. Annie climbed out on her side, opened the back passenger door and reached for the two grocery bags on the seat.

Alex stopped to stretch, taking in the view behind the house where lush evergreens stood outlined against a deep blue sky so clear and close it looked as if he could reach up and touch it.

He could get used to more time off like this. Even though he'd come home because of a serious medical emergency, he was thankful for the break from his stress-filled days at work. The thought of returning to his job and solitary life in San Francisco didn't have the same pull it had those first few days he'd been back in Fairhaven.

Something was changing. Maybe it was him.

He glanced at Annie as she walked around to the trunk. She already juggled two heavy bags, and she was reaching for another.

"Hey, let me take one of those. You go on inside, and I'll get the rest."

She looked up at him, and her lips curved into a grateful smile. "Thanks."

"No problem." His chest expanded with hopeful feelings. He grabbed four bags, then followed Annie as she trotted up the steps and into the house. It was funny how such a simple offer to carry in a few groceries could spark such a positive response. He'd have to remember that.

Then the reason for Annie's reaction hit him. She'd been on her own for a long time, raising her daughter by herself and doing just about everything else without any help. She obviously appreciated someone sharing the load. Well, she deserved a break. And he was glad to give it to her.

It took him two more trips out to the car to bring in the rest of the groceries, but he didn't mind. He set the last three bags on the kitchen table. "Here you go. That's everything."

She took a loaf of bread from one of the bags and sent him a sweet smile. "Thanks, Alex."

"Glad to help." He looked around. "What else can I do?"

"Do you have that receipt? I want to keep it with the rest."

"Sure." He reached in his pocket, pulled out his cell phone and set it on the kitchen table, but he didn't find the receipt. He searched his other pockets and came up empty-handed. "I must've left it in the car."

"That's all right. I'll get it later."

"No, I'll be right back." Humming a tune, he walked out the door and down the steps.

Annie watched Alex stroll outside. He seemed different today—more relaxed and not nearly as tied to his schedule as usual.

And the even bigger surprise was that he actually seemed to enjoy grocery shopping with her. Their trip to the store felt almost like a date as they laughed, talked about past Thanksgivings and planned ways to make the holiday special for Irene. Their friendship seemed to be deepening a little more each day.

The encounter with Brianna had certainly been interesting. She smiled, remembering the way Alex had been turned off by Brianna's overt flirting. Most men would be flattered if an attractive blonde made her interest that obvious. But Alex was not impressed, and that boosted her opinion of him even higher.

Alex's cell phone rang and vibrated on the kitchen table. Annie pushed a sack of groceries aside and glanced at the phone. The photo of a pretty redhead flashed on the screen, along with the name Tiffany Charles.

Annie's heart clenched. Was she the person who'd called him several other times? He always left the room when he answered his phone, and he never talked about those calls.

She stood on tiptoe and glanced out the window over the sink, but she didn't see Alex. He must still be searching for the receipt.

The incessant ringing continued, and the urge to find out more about Tiffany Charles grew stronger. She picked up the vibrating phone, staring at the photo of the redhead with bright blue eyes.

The back door opened. Alex walked in.

Annie jumped and almost dropped the phone. Her hand shot out. "Your phone is ringing."

He frowned slightly, took the phone and glanced at the screen. His eyes flashed, then his expression returned to neutral. "Excuse me a minute." He walked out of the kitchen and down the hall.

She tiptoed to the kitchen doorway and strained to listen while her heart thumped in her chest. But Alex's voice grew distant, and she couldn't make out his words.

Whoever Tiffany Charles was, Alex certainly seemed to want to keep her a secret.

A warning flashed through her mind: *Beware—heartache ahead. Turn back now before it's too late.*

She groaned and closed her eyes. *Is that warning from You, Lord, or is it just my old fears raising their ugly heads?*

Alex walked into the living room and answered the call. He didn't want Annie to worry about his problems at work. "Hey, Tiffany. What's up?"

"Alex, we've got a real situation here."

He frowned. "What's going on?"

"Eric walked out, and Andrea is threatening to do the same."

His stomach took a nosedive. "Eric quit?"

"That's right. The whole team is falling apart."

"Does he have another job offer? Is that why he's leaving?"

"I don't know. All he told me is he's not going to sit around and wait for the merger to go through. He said he'd rather quit than be laid off. And now Andrea is freaking out and threatening to leave."

Alex paced to the window and rubbed his forehead. "Do you think Eric has an inside source?"

"How should I know? No one tells me anything!"

"Okay, I know you're upset, but listen—"

"I'm not just upset. I'm about ready to have a nervous breakdown!" Her voice rose to a high-pitched squeak, then dropped to a pleading whine. "You've got to come back, Alex. I can't deal with all this on my own."

He closed his eyes and pinched the bridge of his nose as he tried process the situation. "I know these past couple weeks have been difficult for you."

"Ha! *Difficult* doesn't even come close to what I'm feeling right now. Please, Alex, can't you just get on a plane and fly back here today?"

He glanced at his watch, checking the date, then shook his head. "It's not going to help for me to fly back on a Friday night. We can't do anything over the weekend. And lots of people are taking next week off because of Thanksgiving."

"Not me. I'll be right here trying to hold everything together until you decide to come back."

"I appreciate that."

She huffed.

"Look, I know it's tough to handle this on your own, but I don't think it will make any difference if I come back now or after Thanksgiving."

She blew out a long breath. "I suppose you're right. Between people taking vacation days and other people quitting, there won't be too many of us in the office next week."

"I'm sure no one is making any decisions until after the holiday. Just hold down the fort a few more days."

"All right, but just so you know, we're not getting much work done around here. You can't expect people to be productive when they're worried about losing their jobs and their medical insurance. Most of us have spouses and kids and bills and mortgages…"

He held the phone a few inches away from his ear until she finished. "I'm sorry. I know this is not what you expected when I asked you to handle things for me. But it won't be much longer, I promise." He hoped to soothe her ruffled feathers with his gentle tone.

"I guess we'll survive. I just can't promise anyone will be here when you finally get back."

"Just try to keep a lid on things. I'll be there in a few days, and we'll get this all straightened out. Okay?"

"Sure. Fine. Enjoy your holiday." Her sarcastic, pouty tone negated her words.

He ended the call and slipped the phone back into his

pocket. Rubbing his forehead, he tried to sift out the facts from Tiffany's tidal wave of emotion.

All he really knew was he'd lost one of his best coworkers, and the rest of the team at Tremont was anxious about the possibility of losing their jobs. If only he could find out what was really going on with the merger—but that was impossible. That kind of news was always kept under wraps until the official announcement was made. How long would he have to wait?

What if Eric was right? What if his job was going to be eliminated? Maybe he should think about starting his own job search.

He lowered his head and closed his eyes. *Lord, I have no idea what's really going on, but I care about my friends. Most of them have families to support, and losing their jobs right now would be really tough. Please watch over this situation. Help me prepare for whatever is coming. And about the bakery, could you please show me what's best for Gram... and for Annie?*

He lifted his head, the burden feeling a little lighter. Taking his questions and struggles to God was becoming a new habit. His grandmother would be proud. Annie would be pleased, too. But even more important than that, he had discovered it was a relief to share his problems with someone who actually had the wisdom and ability to do something about them...and that was the best reason to pray, after all.

"Look, Mom, I ate all my pancakes." Emma grinned and pointed to her empty plate.

Annie turned from washing dishes at the sink. "Good for you, sweetie."

Emma's sticky grin and dancing eyes were too hard to resist. Annie wiped her hands on a towel, then walked over and wrapped her arms around her daughter. Emma smelled like sweet maple syrup and spicy cinnamon.

"Can I have some more?"

Annie chuckled and stepped back. "You're not full yet?"

"No. I've still got lots of room."

"Okay." Annie slid two more small pancakes on Emma's plate, then watched while her daughter squeezed on the maple syrup. "That's enough."

Emma reluctantly put the syrup down. Pancakes were a treat reserved for Saturday morning when they didn't have to rush off to school or church. And it was a good thing, considering the way Emma loved to pour on the toppings.

Irene pushed her half-eaten bowl of oatmeal aside and stared at the newspaper with a wistful look in her eyes.

Alex breezed in and gave his grandmother a kiss on the check. "Morning, Gram. How are you feeling today?"

Irene looked up and sent him a small smile. "I'm fine." But her shoulders sagged as her gaze returned to the newspaper.

Alex cocked his head and sent Annie a questioning glance.

She walked back to the table. "Can I get you something else, Irene?"

"No, thank you, dear." Irene quietly folded the newspaper.

Alex took a plate from the cabinet and returned to the table. "What's wrong, Gram?"

"It's silly, really. I shouldn't let it bother me."

Alex sat in the chair next to her. "What is it?"

"Today is the last day of the Home for the Holidays Gift Show." Irene pointed to the photo on the front page. "The girls and I usually go every year, then we always go out to lunch after. But they didn't invite me this year." Irene blinked a few times and quickly glanced away.

"What's a gift show?" Emma asked, licking the syrup off her fingers.

"It's like a craft fair." Annie patted Emma's shoulder.

"Please take your dishes to the counter and go wash your hands."

"Okay." Emma hopped up and set her plate and silverware by the sink, then headed toward the bathroom.

Alex drummed his fingers on the table. "Maybe your friends decided not to go this year."

"Oh, they're going. We always go. It's tradition."

Alex sent Annie a silent request for help.

She gave a slight nod and took a seat across from Irene. "I'm sure they didn't mean to exclude you. Maybe they just thought that kind of outing might be too much for you right now."

Irene sniffed. "They could've at least asked and given me a chance to say no."

"Why don't you call them, Gram? See if they've made plans yet."

"I can't do that."

"Why not? There's no reason you couldn't go out with your friends for a little while."

"They'll walk around all morning, and I wouldn't be able to keep up. That's probably why they didn't ask me." Irene glanced at the paper again. "It's on the second floor at the Cruise Terminal. I'd never be able to climb all those stairs."

"I'm sure there's an elevator. Public places like that have to be handicap accessible," Annie said.

"You could use the wheelchair we borrowed from Lucile," Alex said.

Irene huffed and drew herself up. "I don't intend to use that thing!"

"Even if it means you could spend the day with your friends and enjoy the gift show?" Alex asked.

"I'd rather stay home than be treated like an invalid in a wheelchair."

Alex crossed his arms. "That's too bad. It sounds like a

nice way to spend a Saturday." Alex looked at Annie, his blue eyes twinkling. "Maybe I should go check it out."

Irene gasped. "You'd go and leave me home?"

Alex suppressed a grin. "Well, if you don't want to go, what can I do?"

Irene narrowed her eyes. "Oh, you stinker. You're teasing me!"

He laughed. "Gram, call your friends and work out the details. You don't have to sit at home and miss out on something you really want to do."

"Well, I suppose I could talk to Barb and find out when they're going."

"Good idea." He got up and walked over to the phone.

"But what if they say yes, and then I get all tired out before they're finished?"

Alex thought for a few seconds. "Why don't we all go?"

Annie's pulse leaped. Alex wanted to take her and Emma to the gift show?

"You can walk around with your friends as long as you want," Alex said. "If you get tired, I'll either take you home or, if you're really feeling brave, I can bring the wheelchair along in the trunk." He looked at Annie and lifted one eyebrow. "What do you say? You and Emma want to come along on this adventure?"

She smiled and nodded, a warm, happy feeling flowing through her. "It sounds like fun."

Christmas lights and shimmering snowflakes twinkled all around the ceiling of the Alaska Cruise Terminal. Christmas music played softly in the background, setting a festive mood for the Home for the Holidays Gift Show.

Alex looked over his shoulder and spotted his grandmother a few booths back, encircled by her friends Hannah, Barb and Marian. They'd stopped to admire a display of antique dishes, floral wreaths and table linens in rich harvest colors.

"Looks like she's having a good time," Annie said.

"Hope so." He paused, concern for Irene shadowing his thoughts.

Annie gently laid her hand on his arm. "I'm sure getting out of the house and spending time with them will lift her spirits."

He glanced back at Annie, surprised she seemed to read his thoughts so easily.

Emma reached for her mother's hand. "What are those?" She pointed to the next booth, where handmade soaps were displayed in gift baskets. They stopped to sniff the soap and squeeze out a sample of lotion.

Alex's thoughts shifted to his grandmother again. They had taken her to the cardiologist yesterday. After the appointment, he'd pulled the doctor aside and told him he was concerned about his grandmother's mood.

The doctor's words played through his mind again. *"It's normal for your grandmother to feel depressed after a heart attack, especially considering all the lifestyle changes she needs to make now that she's home from the hospital."*

Maybe it was normal, but it was still hard for him to see her so down in the dumps.

His stomach tensed as he thought of what lay ahead. He only had a few more days of vacation left, and he was beginning to realize that lining up help with meals and home care might not be enough to see Gram through all the changes she was facing.

But what could he do? Staying in Fairhaven wasn't an option. He had an apartment and a job waiting for him in San Francisco—at least he hoped he still had a job.

"Look at all the hats!" Emma tugged on Annie's hand, pulling her toward the next booth.

He followed them to the display of handmade hats in every size, shape and color you could imagine. They filled the table and metal display racks surrounding it. He grinned as he studied the clever designs.

"Isn't that one cute?" Annie pointed to a kid's felt hat that looked like a Christmas tree, complete with colorful ornaments and a yellow star on top.

"It sure is." He fingered a red plaid fleece hat with earflaps. "Look at this one. I bet that would keep you warm."

Annie smiled and nodded, then shifted her gaze to a jewel-tone knit hat made from a soft fuzzy yarn. It had a brim and three flowers made of the same yarn attached to the side. It would probably look great with her dark hair and eyes. He smiled, picturing it in his mind.

Annie tipped her head and examined the hat for a few more seconds.

"I like this one." Emma reached for a blue-and-brown knit hat with a teddy-bear design on the part that came to a long point in the back. It had a fuzzy pompom tassel on the end.

"Remember, look with your eyes, not your hands," Annie warned her.

Emma bit her lip and slowly lowered her hands to her sides.

The woman working at the booth came around the end of the table. "She can try on the hat if she'd like. I'll get a mirror."

Emma looked up at Annie for permission, and Annie nodded. Emma grinned as she took the teddy-bear hat off the hook and tugged it on her head.

"We call that a toboggan style," the woman said. "It's actually made from a child's sweater." She passed the hand mirror to Emma. "How do you like it?"

Emma caught her reflection in the mirror, and her eyes

lit up. Dimples creased her cheeks. She turned to Alex and looked up at him. "How do I look?"

Suddenly Alex's heart felt like butter melting in a warm pan. He reached out and tapped the end of her nose. "You look great. That's the perfect hat for you."

Emma gazed at herself in the mirror again and ran her hand over the fleece band. "It's so soft." She turned to her mother with pleading eyes, but she didn't voice her request.

Annie checked the price tag, then touched her daughter's cheek gently and shook her head. She took the mirror from Emma and handed it back to the woman. "Thanks for letting her try it on."

Emma slowly took off the hat and hung it up with a resigned sigh.

Alex glanced from Annie to Emma and to the woman selling the hats. He didn't want to overstep his bounds, but Emma obviously loved the hat. When Annie and Emma moved to the other side of the booth, he peeked at the price tag.

It wasn't an outrageous price, but he knew Annie was on a tight budget. It would be hard for her to spend money for something that wasn't a necessity.

"I have an online store." The woman passed him her business card, then lowered her voice. "Maybe you could surprise your daughter and give her the hat for Christmas."

He opened his mouth, intending to say Emma wasn't his daughter. But something stopped him. He thanked her, slipped the card in his pocket and walked over to Annie.

"What did she say?"

He glanced away and pretended he was interested in a green felt trapper hat. "She just gave me her card."

She studied him for a moment, then reached out to touch a burgundy velvet hat. "What will you do with that?"

He gave a slight shrug. "She has an online store. I thought I might buy that hat for Emma…for Christmas."

Annie's hand stilled, and she looked up at him. "Oh, Alex, you don't have to do that."

"I know, but she really liked it."

Annie's smile warmed. "That's sweet of you."

"I remember what it was like when I was a kid and I'd set my heart on something." His gaze traveled to Emma.

She stood a few feet away looking at some other hats. She'd tucked her hands in her pockets, probably as a reminder to obey her mom and not touch anything. She squatted down to get a better look at a pink hat with a fuzzy faux-fur band, a look of curiosity on her face.

"You're lucky, Annie," he said softly. "She's a special little girl."

"Thanks." Tenderness filled Annie's eyes. "But it's not luck. Emma's a blessing. And not a day passes that I don't thank God for sending her into my life."

Alex shifted his gaze to Annie, taking in the sweetness of her expression and the sincerity in her eyes. That was a powerful statement, considering she was a single mom struggling to launch her career and provide for herself and her daughter.

His heart lifted, and a quiet assurance filled his thoughts. Annie wasn't the only one who was blessed. He'd been touched in a special way by her kind and caring ways. And every day, in so many ways, he was beginning to see what a blessing she was to him.

Pastor James closed his Bible and led the congregation in a final prayer. Alex lowered his head and shut his eyes, soaking in the quiet strength of the man's words.

His message this morning made a lot of sense. The clear, practical teaching from the book of Luke reminded him what was important in life, like growing in his faith and strengthening his relationships with God and people.

Once again he realized how far his priorities had shifted away from that. Until he made this trip home to Fairhaven, he'd been totally focused on getting ahead in his career and hadn't given much thought to the needs of anyone other than himself. He pondered that for a moment, trying to understand why he'd taken that path.

Maybe focusing on work was easier than going deeper with God and people. Deeper relationships required commitment and opened one up to the possibility of loss—and that was a risk he didn't take lightly, not after all the losses he had suffered in the past. Still, he sensed his heart opening to new possibilities.

The musicians returned to the platform and the congregation stood to sing a final song. He glanced past his grandmother at Annie, taking in her profile. She closed her eyes as she sang, and the sweetest expression filled her face. His throat tightened, and he had to look away. Watching her open her heart in worship seemed too private and personal.

He focused on the large screen in front and read the words, joining in the song, but he couldn't keep his gaze from drifting back to Annie. She obviously had a deep connection with God. Her face practically glowed with peace and pleasure as she sang.

Suddenly he felt his grandmother watching him. Their gazes connected, and she sent him a slight nod and knowing smile.

He quickly shifted his gaze away. Was Irene aware of his attraction to Annie, or was she suggesting he ought to take a lesson from her devotion?

Either way, he needed to be more careful.

The song ended, and he gathered his coat and stepped out of the pew, followed by Irene and Annie. Before they reached the foyer, Irene's friends surrounded her, excited to welcome her back to church.

Annie tapped his arm. "I need to go pick up Emma."

He nodded. "We'll meet you in the foyer." He watched Annie walk away, admiring the way her dark curls swung across her back with each graceful step.

He shifted his gaze away, reminding himself he needed to keep his thoughts in line, but it was hard when someone as attractive as Annie was around.

Five minutes later he waited for Irene and Annie in the foyer. Annie appeared first with Emma in tow, then Irene walked out the door of the sanctuary.

"Alex, do you remember Jason Hughes?" Irene ushered his former high-school teammate toward him. His tall, husky friend hadn't changed much in ten years. He still had the same light brown hair, gray-green eyes and suntanned face.

Alex shook Jason's hand. "Good to see you."

"Thanks. Good to see you, too. You look great."

Alex chuckled. "I'd look better if I still played basketball the way we used to."

Jason grinned. "Yeah, I hear you." He placed his hand on the shoulder of the little girl beside him. "This is my daughter, Faith." Her long black hair and exotic Asian features implied she was adopted.

They all greeted Faith, then Irene motioned toward Annie. "This is our friend Annie Romano and her daughter, Emma."

Annie smiled and shook hands with Jason.

His eyes brightened as his gaze traveled over her. "Nice to meet you."

A warning flashed through Alex. Jason was making his interest a little too obvious for his comfort. Besides, he must have a wife. He glanced at Jason's left hand, but there was no ring on his finger. Well, not every guy wore a ring. Maybe in his line of work it didn't make sense.

"Is your wife here with you?" Alex asked. Maybe a little reminder would help keep Jason in line.

Jason's expression hardened, and he shook his head. "No, my wife isn't a part of our family anymore."

His grandmother pursed her lips and sent Alex a reproachful look. There was obviously more to the story, but this wasn't the time for it.

"I think Emma and Faith are in the same Sunday school class," Annie said.

Jason's expression softened. "That's great." Pride and affection filled his face as he looked at his daughter. "Faith just turned five last week. How about Emma?"

"Her fifth birthday was in August."

The little girls smiled, looking shy but definitely interested in each other.

"Jason is a contractor." Irene leaned toward Alex. "I was telling him about our plans for remodeling the bakery, and he said he'd be willing to come by and take a look at the building and give us some estimates."

Alex glanced at Annie and back at Jason. "I'm not sure we're ready for that yet." The idea of working with Jason on the project didn't sit right with him.

Jason held up his hand. "There's no obligation. I'll just take a look and run some numbers. It won't bother me if you decide to go with someone else."

"We're still working on the business plan, and we don't have all the financing in line yet."

"That's okay. Maybe if you show me what you've worked out so far I can help you finalize your plans and give you an idea how much it will cost to finish the project."

"That's certainly a nice offer," Irene added, sending Alex a pointed look. "Thank you, Jason."

"I've got some time tomorrow afternoon if you want me to stop by, say one o'clock?"

Get 2 Books FREE!

Love Inspired® Books,
a leading publisher of inspirational romance fiction, presents

A series of contemporary love stories that will lift your spirits and reinforce important lessons about life, faith and love!

FREE BOOKS!
Get two free books by acclaimed, inspirational authors!

FREE GIFTS!
Get two exciting surprise gifts absolutely free!

2 FREE BOOKS

▲ To get your 2 free books and 2 free gifts, affix this peel-off sticker to the reply card and mail it today!

LI-LA-12C

We'd like to send you two free books to introduce you to the Love Inspired® series. Your two books have a combined cover price of $11.50 or more in the U.S. and $13.50 or more in Canada, but they are yours to keep absolutely FREE! We'll even send you two wonderful surprise gifts. You can't lose!

Her Homecoming Cowboy
Debra Clopton

The Doctor's Devotion
Cheryl Wyatt

Lakeside Family
Lisa Jordan

And Father Makes Three
Kim Watters

The Rancher's Secret Wife
Brenda Minton

Each of your **FREE** books is filled with joy faith and traditional values as men and women open their hearts to each othe and join together on a spiritual journey.

GET 2 FREE BOOKS!

Love Inspired

YES! Please send me the 2 FREE Love Inspired® books and 2 free gifts for which I qualify. I understand that I am under no obligation to purchase anything further, as explained on the back of this card.

affix free books sticker here

❏ I prefer the regular-print edition
105/305 IDL FNSH

❏ I prefer the larger-print edition
122/322 IDL FNSH

Please Print

FIRST NAME

LAST NAME

ADDRESS

APT.#   CITY

STATE/PROV.   ZIP/POSTAL CODE

The Reader Service – Here's How it Works:

Accepting your 2 free books and 2 free mystery gifts (gifts valued at approximately $10.00) places you under no obligation to buy anything. You may keep the books and gifts and return the shipping statement marked "cancel." If you do not cancel, about a month later we will send you 6 additional books and bill you just $4.49 each for the regular-print edition or $4.99 each for the larger-print edition in the U.S. or $4.99 each for the regular-print edition or $5.49 each for the larger-print edition in Canada. That's a savings of at least 22% off the cover price. It's quite a bargain! Shipping and handling is just 50¢ per book in the U.S. and 75¢ per book in Canada.* You may cancel at any time, but if you choose to continue, every month we'll send you 6 more books, which you may either purchase at the discount price or return to us and cancel your subscription. *Terms and prices subject to change without notice. Prices do not include applicable taxes. Sales tax applicable in N.Y. Canadian residents will be charged applicable taxes. Offer not valid in Quebec. All orders subject to credit approval. Books received may not be as shown. Credit or debit balances in a customer's account(s) may be offset by any other outstanding balance owed by or to the customer. Please allow 4 to 6 weeks for delivery. Offer available while quantities last.

▼ If offer card is missing write to: The Reader Service, P.O. Box 1867, Buffalo, NY 14240-1867 or visit www.ReaderService.com ▼

BUSINESS REPLY MAIL

FIRST-CLASS MAIL   PERMIT NO. 717   BUFFALO, NY

POSTAGE WILL BE PAID BY ADDRESSEE

THE READER SERVICE

PO BOX 1867

BUFFALO NY 14240-9952

NO POSTAGE
NECESSARY
IF MAILED
IN THE
UNITED STATES

"Wonderful!" Irene clasped her hands under her chin. "I've been praying God would send us some help and keep us moving in the right direction."

Annie nodded. "The sooner we get started, the sooner we can reopen."

Jason sent Annie an appreciative smile. "Great. I'll see you tomorrow at one at the bakery."

"We'll all be there," Irene added with a cheery smile.

Alex stifled a groan. Jason seemed awfully eager to offer his advice on the project. Maybe he was short of work and hoping for a contract, or maybe it had more to do with the way he was eyeing Annie. Either way, it looked as if Alex had been outvoted and outmaneuvered by his grandmother and Annie—again. Whether he liked it or not, they'd be meeting with Jason tomorrow.

Chapter Ten

Annie took Irene's arm and watched Alex pull away from the curb in front of the bakery. He had dropped her and Irene off, saying he'd drive around the block and park in back since there were no parking spaces close by.

Something was definitely bothering Alex. He'd been quiet and tense all morning, and that slight crease between his eyebrows was beginning to look like a permanent feature.

Was he worried about the unknown factors in their business plan? Did he think his grandmother was taking on too much too soon? Or was it something else? There was no way of knowing unless Alex decided to confide in her, and so far he'd kept whatever it was to himself.

A pang of disappointment shot through her heart. She thought they'd been growing closer, but apparently she was wrong.

Fine. She could deal with that. In fact, it was probably for the best. There was no sense opening up to each other and deepening their friendship when he would be leaving soon for San Francisco.

She put those thoughts aside, pulled open the door and escorted Irene into the bakery. The bell jingled overhead, and the aroma of fresh-baked bread and coffee brewing greeted them.

Janelle Crandall, Irene's assistant at the bakery, placed a tray of doughnuts on the counter. "Oh, my goodness, look who's here!" The plump redhead rushed around the bakery case and wrapped Irene in a tight hug. Janelle's twinkly blue eyes squeezed shut, and a look of pure delight filled her face.

Seeing the affection between the two women lifted Annie's spirit.

Janelle finally let go of Irene and stepped back. "It's so good to see you. How are you feeling?"

"I'm coming along. Still a little tired, but each day I'm feeling stronger. The doctor says I can start the cardiac rehab program next week."

Janelle grinned and patted Irene's shoulder. "Good for you."

Harry walked in from the kitchen wearing his black ball hat and white apron over his clothes. He wiped his hands on a towel and greeted Irene with another hug. "Look at you, all fresh and new."

Irene chuckled. "Well, I don't know about that, but at least I'm on my feet and walking around."

Alex came in the back door, passed through the kitchen and joined them. That worried crease still marked the area between his eyebrows as he looked around the bakery. His gaze connected with Annie's for a split second then moved away.

A nervous quiver passed through Annie's stomach. She wished he'd tell her what was wrong. Maybe he would've if there'd been more time to talk this morning, but Irene had been with them since breakfast.

Irene clasped her hands in front of her heart and looked around the group. "I have some good news." Harry and

Janelle watched her expectantly. "We're moving ahead with our plans to remodel the bakery."

"Yes!" Harry pumped his fist in the air.

"Oh, I just knew you wouldn't close us down." Janelle danced over and hugged Irene again.

"We may have to close for a few weeks, but that's so we can give Jameson's a brand-new look and menu." She glanced at her watch, then looked out the front window. "Jason Hughes, a contractor from my church, should be here any minute. He's going to look at our plans and then give us an estimate on the job."

"So he'll be the one to hire all the workmen and oversee everything?" Janelle asked.

Irene nodded. "That's right."

Alex held up his hand. "We're not sure about that yet. We're looking for his input as a professional, someone who can help us evaluate the costs and feasibility of the project. We haven't decided we're going to hire him yet."

"That's true," Irene said. "But I have a very good feeling about this. I checked with a few people, and everyone I talked to praised his work."

Alex's frown deepened, and he crossed his arms. "Who did you call?"

"Pastor James. He said Jason has overseen several jobs for families in the church, and he'd never heard anything but positive reports."

Alex huffed. "Of course he's going to say that. He's a pastor. He can't pass on negative reports about people."

Annie pressed her lips together as her gaze darted from Alex to Irene. Alex's intensity was making her uncomfortable, and no doubt it was doing the same to Irene. She sent Alex a warning look, but he didn't seem to notice.

Janelle brushed some crumbs off one of the tables. "So what kind of changes do you want to make?"

Irene took the file from her bag and laid it on the table in front of Harry and Janelle. "We want to update everything and give the bakery a whole new look. We'll keep the name, but call it Jameson's Bakery Café. Wait until you see these photos."

Alex motioned Annie to follow him across the room while Irene flipped through the pages, showing Harry and Janelle the plans.

Annie met Alex by the bakery case. He leaned closer. "We've got to slow my grandmother down." His urgent whisper sent a tremor through her.

"Why? What's wrong?"

"I'm not comfortable with the idea of hiring Jason."

"Why not? Have you heard something negative about him?"

"No, I just don't think we should move so fast. We don't know anything about the guy."

"I thought he was an old friend of yours."

"We played basketball together ten years ago. That's all. I have no idea what he's been doing since then. And why didn't he explain what happened to his wife?"

"Probably because his daughter was standing there. But how does that have any bearing on his work as a contractor?"

"The way people handle their personal life says a lot about their character."

"Well, he goes to Grace Chapel, and one of the pastors recommends him. That sounds like a pretty good character reference to me."

Alex rubbed his chin. "Maybe. But I'd like to hear from some people who've actually hired him." He leaned closer. "Who knows? The guy could be a crook."

Annie stifled a gasp. "Alex, I can't believe you'd say that."

"Hey, I'm just trying to look out for my grandmother. I

won't be here, and I want to be sure we hire someone who's trustworthy."

Annie's stomach clenched. She might not agree with everything Alex said, but one thing was true: he wouldn't be around during the renovation project. She and Irene would be the ones dealing with whomever they chose as the contractor. That was a big responsibility.

The bell jingled as the door swung open. Jason walked in, wearing a brown suede jacket and well-worn jeans and carrying a clipboard. "Afternoon, friends." He nodded to Irene, then turned his warm smile toward Annie. "How are you doing?"

"I'm fine," she said, returning his smile.

Alex leaned closer. "Remember, this is just an estimate. Don't make any commitments."

She pulled in a deep breath and nodded, but she didn't look him in the eye.

Emma pointed to a drawing of a turkey on the bulletin board of her kindergarten classroom. "That's mine, way up there by the top." She turned to Alex. "Can you get it for me?"

"Are we supposed to take it down?" he asked.

Emma bobbed her head. "My teacher said we could take it home after the program."

"Okay, here you go."

She glanced at the drawing for a second then handed it to her mom.

Annie examined the picture. "I like the way you colored all the feathers."

"Good job, Emma." He took a sip of warm apple cider, savoring the sweet, spicy drink.

Coming with Annie to Emma's Thanksgiving program had stirred up old memories. He hadn't been in a kindergarten classroom since he'd walked out of his own twenty-four years ago. But not much had changed.

Rolling carts piled high with wooden building blocks and Tinkertoys sat by the play area. Low bookshelves filled with a large collection of picture books lined one wall. He even saw a few titles he remembered. In the corner, a round table featured a collection of rocks, pinecones, plants and a fish tank with several goldfish. Colorful finger paintings covered the doors of the coat closet.

He could see why Emma loved coming to school. The room had a happy, busy feeling, and he imagined a lot of creative learning happened here every day.

"You're becoming quite an artist." Annie slipped her arm around her daughter's shoulders.

"Mrs. Carlton said my turkey was good."

"She's right." Annie grinned and tapped Emma on the nose. "We'll have to add it to our Thanksgiving decorations."

"Can we put it on the table?"

Alex chuckled. "I think Gram would like that."

"When are we going to make pumpkin pie?" Emma asked.

"We'll work on that later today."

"Good." Emma looked around the room. "Can I get another cookie?"

"All right." Annie gave her an indulgent smile.

"Bring me one, too," Alex called. "I like those ginger-snaps."

Emma looked over her shoulder and smiled at him, then headed for the refreshment table.

Alex chuckled and shook his head. "She is something else."

Mrs. Carlton, Emma's teacher, wove her way through the crowd toward them. "Hello, Mrs. Romano. Good to see you again." She turned and smiled at Alex, then held out her hand. "Mr. Romano, I'm so glad you could come. Emma has told us so much about you."

Alex blinked and opened his mouth, but his reply stuck in his throat. His gaze darted to Annie.

Her face flamed crimson. "Oh…I should've made the introductions. This is our friend Alex Jameson. He's not Emma's father."

Confusion flashed in Mrs. Carlton's eyes. "I'm sorry. You look exactly the way Emma described her father."

Annie lifted her hand to her throat and adjusted the scarf around her neck. "I'm not sure what Emma told you about her father, but he isn't really involved in her life."

"Oh, dear." The teacher's lips pinched together. "I must've misunderstood what she said. I'm sorry."

"No need to apologize." Annie looked as if she wanted to say more.

But Emma returned carrying a small plate of cookies. She held it out to Alex. "I got two cookies for you."

"Thanks, Emma." He helped himself and took a bite, more to keep his mouth occupied than to enjoy the treat.

"Well, I need to go say hello to some of the other parents." Mrs. Carlton stepped back. "I hope you have a nice Thanksgiving." She gave Annie a serious look. "After the holiday, I'd appreciate it if you give me a call. I'd like to meet with you."

"I'll email you to set up a time."

"That'll be fine." Mrs. Carlton looked down at Emma. "I hope you and your mother have a nice Thanksgiving." But the warmth had gone out of her voice.

"Okay." Emma popped the rest of the cookie in her mouth.

Annie placed her hand on Emma's shoulder. "I think it's time for us to go."

Emma frowned and looked around. "But no one else is going."

Annie steered her daughter toward the coat closet. "I need

to drive Irene to a hair appointment, and we have to bake our pumpkin pie."

"I can take Gram to get her hair done." Alex's gaze connected with Annie's for a second before she looked away. "Sounds like you and Emma could use some time together."

Annie turned away and helped Emma with her coat. "No, I'll take Irene. You have to meet with Harry about the wholesale order."

"I can stop at the bakery after I drop off Gram. She can give me a call when she's done, and I'll pick her up on the way home."

They walked outside in silence and crossed the parking lot to Annie's car. Discomfort swirled through Alex's stomach. Annie was avoiding looking at him, pulling back. Was she afraid he was upset with her, or was she just embarrassed by Emma's comments to her teacher?

Annie opened the back passenger door for Emma. Her daughter hopped up on her booster seat. Annie reached in to help her buckle her seat belt, then shut the door and walked around the back of the car.

Alex followed her. "Annie, wait."

She turned to face him. "I'm sorry…about Mrs. Carlton, and Emma." The vulnerable look in her eyes cut through him. She lowered her head and released a deep sigh. "I'll talk to Emma about it."

His heart contracted. He reached out and lifted Annie's chin. "Hey, it's okay."

Tears gathered in her eyes. "No. It's not. She shouldn't be making up stories about her father."

"She's only five."

"That's no excuse."

"Maybe if you told her the truth, she wouldn't have to make up a story."

Annie froze, her eyes wide. "I can't do that."

"Why not?"

She shook her head and stepped away. "I just can't."

He drew in a deep breath and released it quietly. Would she ever trust him enough to tell him the rest of the story?

Chapter Eleven

Annie scuffed into the kitchen wearing blue fuzzy slippers and carrying her laptop. The delicious scent of pumpkin pie floated in the air as she poured herself a cup of coffee. She sat down at the kitchen table to keep an eye on the pie while it finished baking. She couldn't let it burn, not after she and Emma had worked so hard to roll it, fill it and pinch the edge into perfection.

She glanced toward the hallway and smiled, remembering how Emma had protested going to bed before the pie came out of the oven. But Annie told her she could get up as early as she liked on Thanksgiving morning to see it.

For some reason that worked. Emma settled down, pulled the blanket up to her chin and closed her eyes, looking eager to drift off so morning would hurry up and arrive.

Annie's thoughts shifted to Mrs. Carlton's comments after Emma's class program, and her smile faded. The teacher's assumption that Alex was Emma's father wouldn't have been so bad if Emma hadn't described her father as looking exactly like Alex.

Annie recalled his startled reaction, then cringed and lowered her head into her hands. He must think she'd been hinting to Emma that he'd make a great dad. She couldn't deny that exact idea had run through her mind several times, but she hadn't said a word to Emma.

Was her daughter picking up clues that she had feelings for Alex…or worse yet, was Alex?

She would have to be much more careful and keep her distance over the next four days. Then Alex would leave and the problem would be solved…or would it?

Alex thought she should tell Emma the truth about her father, but he had no idea how difficult that would be. There was no way to frame the story to make it less hurtful or humiliating.

What could she say about Kevin Seagraves? It had been six years since she'd seen him.

The memory of Brianna's comments about Kevin's arrest for embezzlement sent a sick wave of dread through her.

Was it true? Had he really stolen money from his company? Several times she'd been tempted to look for information about him online, but she'd always talked herself out of it…until tonight.

Maybe it was time she found out the truth, but she didn't want Irene or Alex to know.

She tiptoed over to the doorway and peeked through the dining room into the living room. Irene sat in the recliner with her feet up, watching an old musical from the 1950s. Alex was stretched out on the couch reading the newspaper.

She crept back to the table and typed Kevin's name in the internet search box.

Her heart hammered in her ears. Links to several websites popped up on the screen with Kevin's name highlighted. She clicked on the first article from the *Eugene Register-Guard Newspaper.*

A photo of Kevin flashed on the screen, and a soft gasp escaped her lips. He looked much the same, but his hollow-eyed, sorrowful expression sent a chill through her.

The story was dated mid-October, and the headline read Ex-Credit Union Manager Guilty of Embezzlement.

> Kevin Seagraves pleaded guilty to embezzling $687,430 during the last five years while he worked as manager of MELCO Community Credit Union. He expressed regret for his actions and blamed the thefts on a gambling addiction. Seagraves is scheduled for sentencing in Eugene, Oregon, on January seventeenth. The maximum penalty for embezzlement is thirty years of imprisonment and a $1 million fine.

She froze and stared at that last sentence. One million dollars? How would he ever be able to pay a huge fine like that if he was going to spend thirty years in prison? Would the responsibility for paying it fall on his wife's shoulders?

Tears burned in her eyes. When Kevin walked out of her life, she'd been hurt and angry. She had even prayed that God would get a hold of him and make him realize how much he'd hurt her, but she'd never wanted something like this to happen.

Then another thought crashed down on her. What if she'd told him she was pregnant, and he'd come back into her life? What would've happened then? The truth took her breath away. If she'd married Kevin, she'd be right in the middle of this terrible situation...and so would Emma.

Tingles traveled up her arms as that thought sank in. She'd felt so distant from God when she'd gotten pregnant, sure that He'd pulled back from her because He was disappointed in her choices and actions. But He'd been right there all the time, watching out for her and protecting her from deeper heartache. He didn't take away the consequences of her foolish choices, but as soon as she called out to Him, He walked with her in the midst of them and cared for her each step of the way.

She stared at the laptop screen, lost in thought.

"What are you working on?" Alex crossed the kitchen toward her.

She gasped. Her hand shot out, and she closed her laptop.

He stopped and cocked his head. "What's the matter?"

"Nothing." But traitorous heat flooded her face.

He glanced at the closed computer and back at her. "You sure?"

Go ahead. Tell him the truth. Let him read the article and see why you can't tell Emma about her father.

She opened her mouth, but the words wouldn't come.

What would he think of her if he found out Emma's father was a criminal? What did that say about her? She swallowed and pushed those questions away. She couldn't tell him. Not now. "I was just…reading an article online."

He nodded slowly, but she read the disappointment in his eyes, and it about killed her.

He turned away, took a mug from the cabinet and poured himself a cup of coffee, while the silence hung between them like a thick cloud.

Her stomach churned and twisted. What if she told him the truth? Maybe he'd understand, maybe he wouldn't—but hiding this from him was hurting them both.

What should I do, Lord?

The answer came immediately. Still she fought it as she watched him pour cream and sugar into his coffee.

Finally, she blew out a deep breath and slowly opened her computer. "The article was about a guy I dated in college."

His blue eyes lit up, and a slight smile curved one side of his mouth. "Ah, so you were reading about an old flame."

She forced herself to continue. "His name is Kevin Seagraves. He's…Emma's father."

Alex's eyes flashed, then he quickly schooled his expression. "Why's there an article about him online?"

"He's in a lot of trouble." With a trembling hand, she turned the computer toward Alex.

He sat down next to her, focused on the screen and quickly scanned the article. When he finished, he sat back and rubbed his chin, his expression unreadable.

"See why I can't tell Emma about him? What would I say? Oh, yes, you have a father. But he has a gambling addiction, and he's going to prison for embezzlement."

His expression softened. "I'm sorry, Annie. Do you…still have feelings for him?"

Her queasy stomach contracted. "No, not anymore. I haven't seen him since I was nineteen." She pressed her lips together for a few seconds. Finally she said, "He doesn't know about Emma."

Alex blinked. "You never told him?"

"No. We only dated for a few months. Then we broke up, and he moved away before I realized I was pregnant."

"But he could've helped you or at least sent child support."

She looked away and shook her head. "God took care of us. He provided in other ways."

Alex waited quietly, encouraging her with an understanding expression.

"Kevin had serious problems even back then. I never should've gotten involved with him, but I thought I could help him change." She shook her head. "But instead of him changing, I was the one who compromised and ended up pregnant."

So much compassion filled his eyes that she had to look away. "I saw things a lot more clearly after we broke up. I didn't want him involved in Emma's life." She nodded to the computer. "Now I'm sure that was the right decision. When she's older I'll explain things, but not now."

He nodded slowly, his blue eyes shining. "I admire you, Annie."

She sat back and searched his face. "I don't know why. I've made some serious mistakes."

"Hey, you're not the only one who's made mistakes. I've made plenty of them." He sent her a slight grin. "But seriously, I admire the way you've taken a tough set of circumstances and made the best of them."

"I've tried."

"You put yourself through culinary school, and you've raised Emma to be a great kid."

"Who makes up stories about her father."

"Well, you'll probably have to talk to her about that, but overall she's seems happy and well-adjusted. I'm sure she'll be okay, and so will you." He reached over and laid his hand over hers. "Thanks for telling me. I know it wasn't easy." The warmth in his expression and gentle touch of his hand felt like a soothing balm.

"Thanks for listening." She wanted to say more, tell him how much it meant that he didn't criticize or condemn her, but she couldn't get those words out. So she sent him a smile instead, hoping he would see in her eyes what was in her heart.

Chapter Twelve

Alex opened the oven door and peeked inside. The savory scent of roasting turkey floated out on a wave of heat. He pulled in a deep breath, and his mouth watered.

"Hey, what do you think you're doing?" Annie placed her hands on her hips and pretended to scowl, but her dark eyes sparkled with a humorous light.

She sure looked cute in that flowered apron with her hair tied back and that one dark curl swinging free next to her cheek…almost as sweet and delicious as the apple crisp cooling on the counter.

"I'm just checking on the bird. We wouldn't want it to burn," he said, matching her teasing tone.

"Well, every time you open that door, you lower the temperature and mess with the cooking time."

He shut the oven and took a step toward her. "Is that so?"

Her eyes danced, and her face flushed a pretty pink. "Yes, it is."

He tipped his head and sent her a cocky grin. "Well, I guess we'll just have to see what we can do to raise the temperature around here."

Her mouth dropped open, then just as quickly snapped

shut. She spun away, opened the refrigerator and rummaged around in the vegetable drawer for a few seconds.

He chuckled and leaned against the counter. Something had definitely shifted in their friendship. He'd sensed it in the past few days. Then the night before, when Annie shared more about her past, it had drawn them even closer. This new softening and openness on her part made him feel as if there was a huge magnet pulling them together.

He wasn't sure where everything was headed, but he definitely wanted to test the waters and see.

Carrying a load of vegetables, Annie walked over to the kitchen table and pulled red and green peppers out of a plastic bag.

He followed her across the kitchen. "What are you going to make now?"

"I didn't know you were so interested in cooking."

"Sure I am," he added with another cheeky grin. "I like cooking. Especially when you're making the food and I'm eating it."

She laughed and shook her head. "You're funny, you know that?"

He shrugged one shoulder. "I try."

A smile played at the corner of her lips as she set out a wedge of purple cabbage and a head of romaine lettuce. "I'm going to make a Seven Layer Salad. One of my friends from culinary school sent me the recipe."

"So what's in this Seven Layer Salad?"

"It has some different vegetables with shredded cheese and a creamy dressing spread over the top. Then you decorate it with a design made out of colorful peppers. Sort of like a mosaic."

"Sounds good. Maybe I could help you."

"You want to make the salad with me?"

"Sure. I'll be a great assistant. Just tell me what to do."

They laughed and talked as they worked together for the next few minutes. She showed him how to rinse and pat dry the lettuce leaves. Then he followed her directions as he chopped the head of romaine and placed it in the bottom of a cut-glass bowl, along with a second layer of purple cabbage.

"That looks great." She glanced at the recipe. "Next we add a layer of water chestnuts and then some thinly sliced purple onion."

"Water chestnuts?" He lifted one eyebrow. "I've never even heard of them."

She laid the little white circular slices over the purple cabbage in a neat pattern. "They don't have too much flavor, but they add a nice crunch."

He stepped up next to her and leaned over her shoulder, close enough to catch the soft floral fragrance in her hair. It reminded him of walking through a garden on a summer afternoon.

She glanced up at him with a teasing smile. "Here, you can slice this next." She handed him a purple onion.

He set to work, peeling off the wrinkled outside skin and cutting thin slices. Within a few seconds, his nose tingled and his eyes began to burn. He pulled back and squinted against the fumes. "Hey, you didn't tell me this stuff was like pepper spray."

"Hold your breath. That should help."

"Okay." He squeezed the word out through his tight lips, but it was no use. Tears flooded his eyes and overflowed down his face.

"Sorry. I didn't realize you were so sensitive to onions."

"It's okay." He sniffed and grimaced.

Annie grabbed a tissue from the box and held it out to him, but his hands were full and reeking with onion juice, so he used his shoulder in a vain attempt to wipe his face.

He finished the last slice, then coughed and waved his

hand over the salad. "Whew. That's strong stuff." Blinking rapidly, he tried to clear his burning vision.

"Here, let me help." She reached toward him with the tissue and gently wiped the tears from his face.

His heartbeat sped up, and his vision began to clear. At this close range, he had a great view of the dark, feathery lashes surrounding her warm, expressive eyes. His gaze traveled across her pink cheeks and down the gentle slope of her nose, stopping at her full, pink lips.

Her hand stilled. Her lips parted, and he could see her pulse throbbing at the base of her neck.

"Annie," he whispered, then reached for her hand, drew it to his lips and kissed her fingers.

"Alex...I'm not sure we should—"

"Shh." He placed his finger against her lips. "You don't need to be sure about anything right now. Just trust me."

A hint of fear flickered in her eyes.

"I'd never hurt you, Annie. I promise."

Her gaze softened, inviting him closer.

He leaned down until his lips brushed hers, kissing her gently. Her lips were soft and sweet and tasted like cinnamon and sugar. He held back, but it was hard when she responded with warmth and feeling that surprised him.

His senses reeled, and he had to force himself to think past the moment. Finally, he stepped back and pulled in a deep breath. "Wow. That was...amazing."

She blinked a few times. "Yeah." Then she ran her tongue over her lower lip, and her face flushed a deeper pink. "Alex, I don't know. Maybe this isn't such a good idea."

"Hey, it's okay." He moved closer and wrapped her in a hug. Everything in him wanted to wipe the fear and questions from her eyes.

She rested her head against his chest. "But you're leaving in three days. What's going to happen then?"

"We'll figure it out." He willed confidence into his voice, but he had no clear idea about the future.

She pulled away and shook her head. "We shouldn't do this. It's too complicated. I have to think about Emma and the bakery and your grandmother."

He placed his hands on her upper arms, holding her still. "Annie, look at me." He waited until she lifted her gaze to meet his. "You're a beautiful, talented and wonderful woman. I care about you, and I'd be crazy to let a chance for a relationship slip out of my hands just because things are complicated."

Her eyes filled with tears, and her lips trembled. "You're kidding, right?"

"What?" He stared at her for a second, trying to understand what she meant. "No! I'm totally serious." How could she not know how great she was? He grabbed a tissue and held it out to her.

"Sorry I'm so emotional. But it's been a very long time since anyone said something that sweet to me, and I'm just having a little trouble believing you really mean it."

The thought that she'd been hurt before felt like a knife in his heart. He slipped his arm around her shoulder, wishing he could right all the wrongs in her past and somehow make up for the pain she'd experienced. "Of course I mean it. I wouldn't say it if I didn't."

Annie relaxed and leaned against him, then released a shuddering breath.

"Hey, the parade's on TV!" Emma ran into the kitchen and slid across the hardwood floor in her stockinged feet.

Annie straightened and started to pull away, but he kept his arm around her shoulder.

"And my tooth is loose! Look!" Emma opened her mouth and wiggled one of her front lower teeth.

"Wow, look at that." Annie leaned down, and he finally let go of her.

"Nice," Alex said. "You'll have to ask your mom to tell you about the Tooth Fairy."

Emma's eyes brightened. "Tooth Fairy?" She had her own set of wings and a wand and loved anything to do with fairies.

Annie touched Emma's shoulder. "Yes, remind me about that tonight. I'll tell you about her when I tuck you in."

Emma tapped her foot in an impatient rhythm as she looked back and forth between Alex and Annie. "So are you coming to see the parade?"

Annie turned to Alex. "Why don't you go ahead? I'll finish the salad and come in a few minutes."

"Okay." He squeezed her hand and sent her a secretive smile. "We'll save a seat for you." Then he scooped up Emma and flew her back into the living room amid her peals of laughter.

Annie stood by the table as Alex carried Emma out of the kitchen to watch the Thanksgiving parade. Emma spread her arms like a bird and flew into the living room in Alex's arms. The sound of her daughter's laughter echoed back through the house. Then Irene's voice rose above it all, telling Alex to be careful and to put Emma down gently.

Annie's heart swelled, and tears burned her eyes again. What an amazing day this had been.

She hugged herself, replaying the events of the past few minutes. Were they real? Had Alex actually said he thought she was beautiful and talented and worthy of his love? Well, he hadn't actually said the worthy-of-his-love part, but that was what he'd meant, wasn't it?

He'd kissed her. And she'd kissed him back.

She ran her finger over her lips, and the memory of that kiss set her heart pounding again.

But doubts rose and echoed through her mind.

Don't be a fool, Annie. Alex might have good intentions, but he has a job in San Francisco, an apartment and friends there...especially one particular friend named Tiffany.

She bit her lip as uncertainty swirled through her. Closing her eyes, she lifted a prayer. *I don't want to give my heart away again unless Alex is the right man for me. Please show me what to do. If this is not right, make it obvious to me so I can put a stop to it before it's too late.*

But she was afraid her heart had already made up its mind about Alex.

A contented, peaceful feeling settled over Alex as he leaned against the doorjamb of Emma's bedroom, watching Annie tuck her daughter into bed that evening.

Even though it was after nine, his stomach was still full from their delicious Thanksgiving dinner and the great desserts that followed. Annie had done an amazing job adapting several recipes to make healthy options that his grandmother could enjoy.

Celebrating Thanksgiving with Annie, Emma and Irene had been great. After dinner, Irene's Bayside Treasure friends came over for dessert. Who would've thought he'd enjoy playing a rousing game of speed Scrabble with a group of seniors? But he had.

He hadn't even minded the way they watched him and Annie for any signs that their matchmaking hints were working.

He glanced at Annie again, his heart lifting. One small lamp glowed on Emma's bedside table, spreading a cozy circle of golden light around them. Annie folded the soft flannel sheet over the edge of the bedspread and pulled it up to Emma's chin.

With a tender smile, she leaned down and kissed her daughter's forehead.

"Can you tell me about the Tooth Fairy now?" Emma asked, looking up at her mother.

He should've known Emma wouldn't forget what he'd told her after she'd showed them her loose tooth that morning.

"When your tooth falls out, you put it under your pillow," Annie said. "After you go to sleep that night, the Tooth Fairy comes. She takes your tooth and leaves you some money in its place."

"She takes my tooth?" Emma's eyes widened. "Does she give it back?"

"Not usually."

Emma's face puckered. "That's not very nice."

"Well, you don't have to give her your tooth if you don't want to. It's just a game parents play with their kids when they lose a tooth."

"It's a game?"

"Yes, or maybe we should call it a tradition, like the Easter Bunny and Santa Claus."

Emma's expression grew thoughtful. "But they're not real, right?"

Alex straightened. Emma seemed awfully young to know that the Easter Bunny and Santa Claus weren't real.

"That's right," Annie continued. "But we can still play the Tooth Fairy game when you lose your tooth if you'd like."

Emma glanced up at her mom, a slight frown creasing her forehead.

"Hey, who says the Tooth Fairy isn't real?" Alex crossed the room and squatted next to Emma's bed. "She always left me a dollar every time I put a tooth under my pillow."

Emma's eyes grew round as marbles. "A dollar?"

"That's right, a whole dollar."

"Sounds like you had a very generous Tooth Fairy," Annie added, but she didn't sound particularly happy about it.

"That's right. She never let me down." He smiled at Emma. "And as you can see—" he pointed to his teeth "—I had a lot of chances to find out if she'd come."

"Do you think she'll leave me a dollar when my tooth comes out?"

"Sure she will. Just be good and be sure to tuck your tooth under your pillow the day it falls out." Alex patted her shoulder. "She'll know it's there. You'll see."

She smiled up at him, her eyes glowing. "Okay. I will."

"Night, Emma." He smoothed her hair down and stepped back. "Sweet dreams."

Annie kissed Emma once more and followed him out of the room. As soon as they stepped into the hall, Annie motioned him to follow her away from Emma's door.

His heartbeat kicked up in anticipation of another kiss, but when she turned and faced him, the look in her eyes said a kiss was the last thing on her mind.

"Why did you do that?"

"Do what?"

"Try to make Emma believe the Tooth Fairy is real."

He straightened, surprised by the irritation in her voice. "Well…she seems awfully young to give up a fantasy she could enjoy for a few years."

Annie's eyes flashed. "There's a big difference between truth and fairy tales."

"Come on, Annie. What's the harm in believing in the Tooth Fairy, or the Easter Bunny or Santa Claus for that matter?"

"The harm would be confusing her about what's real and what isn't."

"She needs to know that at five years old?"

"Yes, she does." Annie crossed her arms and leveled her steady gaze at him. "I want her to know Jesus is real, and when we read stories about Him in the Bible, I want her to believe those things actually happened."

He tipped his head, conceding her point, but he still felt she was taking this too far. "So you don't do Easter egg hunts? And what about Christmas? Is Santa banned, too?"

Annie bristled. "No, Emma hangs up her stocking and we visit Santa at the mall, but I tell her those are games we play, and I make sure she knows the true reason for the holiday."

"That seems like a lot to expect a five-year-old to grasp."

"She seemed to grasp it just fine until you tried to convince her the Tooth Fairy was real."

"But that's just a fun part of being a kid. It's not going to hurt her."

"Maybe not, but I wish you'd respect my decision and not try to undermine me."

He held up his hands. "Okay. I get it. You've made up your mind." His voice came out harsher than he intended. "I won't mention the Tooth Fairy again."

Hurt reflected in her eyes. "Try to see this from my perspective, Alex. You won't be here to put a dollar under her pillow or fill her Christmas stocking. It's up to me. I'm the only parent she has."

Her words stung, but she was right. Unless he was willing to commit himself to taking on the role of husband and father, he had nothing to say about how she raised Emma.

She turned away and walked toward her bedroom.

"Annie, wait."

She stopped in her doorway and looked back at him. "I'm tired, Alex. This isn't a good time to talk."

He swallowed and nodded. "Okay. We'll talk tomorrow."

But she didn't reply. Instead she stepped into her room and closed her door.

* * *

Alex rolled over onto his side and stared out his bedroom window. The row of pines on the hill behind his grandmother's home rose like tall, black soldiers silhouetted against the midnight sky. Above the treetops, stars winked back at him like tiny flashes of hope.

The kiss he had shared with Annie that morning replayed through his mind for the hundredth time, but the memory was quickly washed away as the conversation about the Tooth Fairy returned in full force. That final look of hurt in Annie's eyes flashed before him again.

He groaned, rolled over and punched his pillow.

Was he crazy? What had he been thinking? He didn't want to lose his chance with Annie over something as stupid as the Tooth Fairy.

Of course, it wasn't stupid to Annie, and it wasn't just the Tooth Fairy. He'd called her parenting skills into question and undercut what she'd been teaching Emma. That was a mistake, one he regretted now. She deserved his respect and support, but he'd laughed at her ideas and blown off her concern.

Would this ruin their chance at a relationship before it even started? What a terrible way to end the day.

He released a deep sigh and lifted his eyes to the ceiling. *Lord, I'm sorry. I really messed things up tonight. Could You help me figure this out?*

He wasn't sure what else to say, but just talking to God about it and admitting he didn't have the answers was a relief. A sense of peace settled over him, and for the first time in a long time, he believed God not only heard his prayer, but that the answer was on the way.

Closing his eyes, he settled into his pillow and drifted off to sleep.

Chapter Thirteen

The doorbell rang a third time as Annie hurried down the hallway the next morning. Who would be coming to the door at nine-fifteen on a holiday weekend?

Annie passed Emma in the living room. Her daughter lay on the rug in her pajamas watching a *VeggieTales* video.

Peeking out the edge of the large oval glass in the front door, she spotted Jason Hughes. Surprise flashed through her, and she quickly pulled open the door and greeted him.

"Morning, Annie." He smiled and held up a file folder. "I have the bid for the bakery renovations ready. I know you want to move quickly on this, so I thought I'd stop by and drop it off." His warm gaze traveled over her, approval glowing in his eyes.

Heat infused her cheeks, and she pushed her damp curls over her shoulder.

His gaze shifted to her drippy hair. "I called and left a message about an hour ago."

"I guess I didn't hear the phone. Sorry."

He held up his hand. "No, I'm the one who should apologize. Would you like me to come back later?"

"No, it's okay. Irene's still resting, and I'm not sure where Alex is, but you can come in." She looked over her shoulder, wishing Alex would appear. Maybe Jason was just a friendly guy, but his admiring glances were making her a little uncomfortable.

"Alex went running." Emma hopped up and joined her in the entryway. She smiled up at Jason. "Where's Faith?"

He grinned at the mention of his daughter. "She's at her aunt Cindy's this morning, hanging out with her cousins and eating French toast with strawberries and whipped cream."

"Mmm, I love French toast." Emma turned to Annie. "Can you make me some?"

"We'll talk about that in a few minutes. Why don't you go get dressed?" She gave Emma a little pat on the back to get her moving.

Emma scampered off toward her bedroom.

"There are a few things I'd like to explain about the bid. Maybe I could go over those with you, and then you could pass that info on to Irene and Alex."

A whisper of unease traveled through Annie. "I think we should wait for Alex to get back."

He tipped his head and smiled. "But you're going to be the new manager, right?"

"Yes, that's true." She rubbed her damp palms on her pants legs, still feeling uncertain.

"I don't think he'll mind. It's all pretty straightforward."

She couldn't think of any other reason to delay him, so she motioned toward the living room. "Okay. Let's sit in here."

Jason settled on the couch while she paused the DVD. He opened the file folder and laid it on the coffee table.

Annie sat next to him, careful to keep some distance between them. She didn't want to send the wrong message or encourage him in any way.

Jason studied her for a moment. Then he launched into his presentation, outlining the phases of the renovation and the different types of workmen he'd hire for each part of the job.

Annie nodded, trying to take it all in, but she didn't have much experience with construction.

"If we can schedule some of the work for late December and the first half of January, we can save quite a bit by hiring college students who'll be home on break. If you're agreeable to that, I have a couple guys in mind who could do the tile and painting."

"Are they experienced?"

He nodded. "I've used them before, and they did a good job for me."

"We do want to save money, but we also want quality work."

"Of course." He grinned. "I'll make sure you get what you pay for and keep the whole job on track. I won't let anyone do shoddy work or cut corners on quality." He paused and sent her a meaningful look. "I'll look out for you, Annie. I promise."

A tremor traveled up her back, and she broke eye contact with Jason. She flipped through the bid again, stopping at the last page. The figure at the bottom was higher than she'd expected, but what did she know about the cost of renovations?

"Do you have any questions?" Jason sat back and stretched his arm out behind her on the couch.

Annie leaned forward and placed the papers on the table. "Not right now, but I'll show it to Irene and Alex and talk it over with them."

"Great." He turned toward her. "I'm looking forward to working on this project with you. I promise I'll give you my best."

Annie forced a small smile, trying to hide her discomfort. "Thanks, Jason."

Alex's feet pounded out a steady beat on the wet pavement as he rounded the corner of Bayside and Willow Road. Fresh, cool air filled his lungs.

He glanced at his watch and picked up the pace. He planned to be back at the house by nine-thirty. Annie should be up by then. He'd ask Irene to watch Emma so he and Annie could have a few minutes alone to talk. He had some important things he needed to say.

When he woke up this morning, the answer to his prayer was clear. He did not want to lose Annie. If he was going to convince her to take a risk on a long-distance relationship, he'd have to make the most of his last two days in Fairhaven. But he was up for the challenge.

He'd show her how much he cared and prove he was a man worthy of her trust and respect. And even though they'd soon be separated by hundreds of miles, their relationship could work.

By next summer, if things were still progressing as he hoped, Annie could move to San Francisco. That would give them more time together and a chance to be sure this was the right relationship for both of them. If that went well, maybe by next Christmas he'd be ready to propose.

Positive energy surged through him. Yes, this was a good plan, one that would make them both happy.

His grandmother's house came into view at the end of the street, and he slowed his pace. But his heart continued to pound. He wasn't sure if it was from the run or the thought of seeing Annie and telling her what he'd been thinking.

He jogged up the driveway and took the front steps two at a time. With his spirits flying high, he pushed open the front door and strode into the house.

He walked into the living room and spotted Annie sitting next to Jason. The brawny contractor had his arm stretched out across the back of the couch only a few inches from Annie's shoulders. Alarm shot through Alex.

Annie's eyes widened. "Alex!"

Jason stood and extended his hand. "Good morning, Alex."

Alex nodded and shook his hand. "Jason."

"I'm headed out of town later today, so I stopped by to drop off the bid." He picked up a folder on the coffee table and offered it to Alex. "I thought you'd want to take a look at it before you fly back to San Francisco."

The reminder that he'd be leaving town while Annie stayed behind hit him again. He clenched his jaw and glanced over the bid, frowning when he saw the total on the last page.

Jason smiled and motioned toward the file. "I always give my friends from church a ten percent discount."

Alex studied the bid a few seconds longer without replying.

"Well, why don't you read it through and then give me a call? My cell number's on there."

Alex nodded.

"If everything looks good to you, we could start working on the exterior right away. The order for the new sign should go in as soon as possible."

Alex closed the folder. "We'll discuss it with my grandmother and get back to you with our decision."

Jason's expression sobered. "Okay, I'll wait to hear from you."

Jason focused on Annie, and his smile returned. "Hope you enjoy the rest of your holiday weekend. We won't be in church on Sunday. I'm taking Faith down to Longview to see her grandparents, but we'll be back Sunday afternoon."

Alex frowned. Why did he think Annie needed to know when he was coming back? Were they making plans to get together after Alex left town? That thought shook him, and he quickly ushered Jason toward the front door.

Annie followed them into the foyer. "Hope you have a nice time with your family."

"Thanks. I'll see you next week." Jason pushed open the screen and stepped outside.

She waved to him. "Bye, Jason."

"Goodbye, Annie." He nodded to Alex, but it looked like an afterthought.

Alex closed the door. "Man, he's sure eager to get this job."

"Yes, he's quite the salesman, very persuasive."

Alex huffed. "Persuasive? It seems more like overconfident and arrogant to me."

"Really?"

"Yes." He shook his head. "Like I said before, I'm not sure I like the idea of working with him."

Annie narrowed her eyes and studied him for a few seconds.

"What?" He lifted his hands, trying to read her expression. "He's acting like he already has the job, but we haven't even hired him."

"I suppose he's trying to show confidence."

"It's more than that. He's obviously got something on his mind other than winning a contracting job."

A faint smile teased the corners of her lips. "Alex Jameson, you sound like you're jealous."

He straightened and shook his head. "I'm not jealous. I just don't like that he's so pushy."

She tipped her head and waited, her slight smile unchanged.

Heat crawled up his neck. "Okay. Maybe I'm a little jealous."

Her smile bloomed, and she took a step closer. "Aw, Alex, don't look so flustered, that's not necessarily a bad thing."

"It's not?"

"No." She slipped her hand into his and gave it a little squeeze. "It's kind of sweet."

Pleasant warmth flowed from her hand up Alex's arm, and his irritation with Jason faded. "Can we talk about last night?"

She nodded, still holding tightly to his hand.

He led her into the living room, and they sat on the love seat. "I'm sorry for what I said. I was out of line. You're doing a great job with Emma."

"Thanks, Alex. That means a lot."

"You deserve my support and encouragement, not some off-the-cuff advice I haven't even thought through."

"It's okay."

"No, I mean it, Annie. I want to do better."

Sweet acceptance filled her eyes. "You know, ever since Emma was born, I've been the only one making decisions about what's best for her. I'm not used to taking parenting advice from anyone else."

He nodded, realizing again how much he admired her for the sacrifices she'd made to love and care for her daughter.

"But that doesn't mean I have it all figured out, or that I don't need help and advice. I do. But last night when you questioned me, I felt defensive and I overreacted."

"But you were right, Annie. It's important for Emma to understand what's true and what's pretend. When I was lying in bed last night, I prayed and God helped me see what's most important."

A look of wonder filled her eyes. "You prayed about it?"

He nodded and smiled. "You and Emma have been wearing off on me."

"That's wonderful, Alex. I'm so happy to hear it."

"I never stopped believing, Annie. I've just had some tough things happen that made me question my faith."

"You mean losing your parents and brother?"

Her insight caught him by surprise, and for a moment he couldn't speak. He swallowed and nodded. "Yeah. I'm still working through that, but watching how you interact with Emma and live out your faith each day is helping me."

Tears shimmered in her eyes. She slipped her arms around him and hugged him tight. "Thanks for sharing that, Alex. That means so much."

"I guess I should've mentioned it sooner and thanked you."

She kissed his cheek, her eyes glowing. "It takes a strong man to admit he needs the Lord's help and guidance."

He cocked his head and grinned. "So you think I'm a strong man?"

She laughed softly. "Definitely."

Chapter Fourteen

Annie plucked a few needles from a Douglas fir as they walked past and lifted them to her nose. The fresh, evergreen scent smelled just like Christmas and put a smile on her face.

This was the first time she'd come to a tree farm to cut a live Christmas tree, and sharing the adventure with Alex and Emma made it even more special.

"How about this one?" Alex lifted his hand to shade his eyes against the late-afternoon sun, then walked around to inspect a giant blue spruce from the other side.

He looked like a handsome lumberjack in his brown jacket, with a knit hat pulled low and a plaid scarf tied around his neck. His leather hiking boots and the trusty handsaw he carried completed the woodsman picture.

Emma tugged on her hand. "Mom, Alex is talking to you."

"Oh. Right." Squinting, she tried to picture the tall spruce in Irene's living room. "That one's very pretty, but don't you think it might be a little too tall?"

Alex rubbed his chin and turned to Emma. "What do you think, Em? Is it too big?"

Her daughter's dark eyes sparkled, and she shook her head. "I like it."

Alex grinned at Annie. "Your call, sweetheart."

Her stomach fluttered like a swirl of dancing snowflakes. No one had ever called her sweetheart, not even her father. "I love the frosty blue-gray color."

"So you like it better than the Douglas fir?"

She looked over her shoulder at the shorter tree they'd tagged as their first choice. "I suppose we could cut off some of the bottom at home if it's too tall."

"Good idea. Gram likes to use evergreen branches to decorate around the house." He lifted the saw and pointed at the tree. "So this is the one?"

Annie checked with Emma, and her daughter gave her a thumbs-up. "That's our tree."

Emma danced around them, her nose and cheeks glowing bright pink.

Alex knelt next to the spruce, while Annie and Emma held the branches up out of his way. In just a few minutes he sawed through the trunk. "Hold tight."

"Timber!" Emma called as the tree broke loose and fell into their waiting arms.

Laughing and teasing each other about how heavy it was, they carried it back to the barn, where the attendant slipped mesh netting over the limbs and helped Alex tie it to the roof of the car.

As they drove back to Fairhaven, they munched on apple-cinnamon doughnuts, sipped hot cocoa and listened to Christmas songs on the radio.

"Oh, look at the lights!" Emma called from the backseat.

Annie laid her hand on Alex's arm. "Let's slow down so she can see."

Alex nodded, then pulled over and parked in front of the Fairhaven Village Green. Lights had been strung over the covered walkway that surrounded the Green on three sides, giving it a twinkling fairyland appearance.

At the far end of the Green, a crowd had gathered in front

of the stage where a group of carolers stood next to a cluster of Christmas trees. Hundreds of tiny white lights sparkled in their branches.

Alex rolled down the windows, and the sweet strains of "Away in a Manger" filled the air.

"I know that song," Emma said and joined in.

Annie's heart swelled as she listened to her daughter sing along. Alex reached for Annie's hand, his gaze warm and tender.

When the song ended, the muted clapping of the crowd drifted back toward them across the Green.

His cell phone rang, and regret filled his eyes. "It could be Gram. We've been gone awhile." He pulled his phone from his pocket and frowned at the screen. "It's my boss. I better take this."

"Sure," Annie said.

"Hey, Steve. How are you?" Alex's brows dipped as he listened. Then he huffed out a breath. "Are you serious? But what about our contracts?" He glanced at Annie, then looked away and rubbed his forehead. "I can't believe this."

Annie's stomach tensed. The carolers started a new song. Alex pushed the button and raised the windows, blocking out the music.

"I heard the rumors, but I didn't expect it to happen so soon." He shifted in his seat, turning away from Annie.

It looked as if Alex wanted some privacy to finish the conversation. "Come on, Emma. Let's go see the lights."

Alex covered the mouthpiece. "You don't have to go."

"We'll be right out here." She unbuckled her seat belt, and she and Emma climbed out of the car.

Annie slipped her hand into Emma's and walked across the grass toward the stage. They listened to another carol, but Annie barely heard the words as Alex's phone conversation replayed through her mind. He was obviously upset about something at work, but what did it mean?

As the next song started, Alex joined them at the back of the crowd.

"Is everything okay?" she asked.

He shook his head, his expression somber. "My company was bought out. They're making the merger announcement on Monday."

Her stomach dropped. "Oh, Alex, what does that mean for you?"

"I'm not sure. My boss is calling everyone in for an emergency meeting tomorrow at noon. I need to head home now and make arrangements."

"You're leaving?" A dizzy wave of panic flooded her mind.

"I have to fly out tonight or first thing tomorrow morning."

"But I thought we'd at least have the rest of the weekend."

"I know. I'm sorry."

Her throat burned, and tears filled her eyes.

"I didn't want to end our time together like this." He pulled her in for a hug, but she remained stiff and unyielding.

See, he's leaving you just like he did before. Just like Kevin and your father did. No matter what they say, this is the way it always ends.

"Annie, please try to understand."

She pulled away from him. "Oh, I understand. What you have in San Francisco is more important to you than what you have here. It makes sense. Don't worry about it." She took Emma's hand and strode toward the car.

"Annie!" He hustled after her. "Listen to me."

"I don't want to hear any more. Let's just go." With a trembling hand she opened the back door for Emma. Her daughter climbed in and looked up at her with wide eyes. Annie helped her with her seat belt.

"Come on, Annie. Don't be mad. That's not fair."

She slammed the door, hoping to keep at least part of the conversation from Emma's ears. "Not fair? I'll tell you what's not fair. You kiss me and tell me how much you care, and then a day later you're ready to take off for who knows how long, with no promise of when you'll be coming back. Tell me about unfair."

"Look, I'm really sorry. I didn't plan this. But if I don't go now, I'll lose my job for sure. Then what kind of future can I offer you?"

She stared at him for a second as those words sank in. "You're thinking about a future for us?"

"Of course I am." He took her hand, sincerity shining in his eyes. "I don't know exactly what's going to happen, but I want us to be together."

Everything in her wanted to believe what he said was true. But could she trust him?

"If they cut my job, I'm coming back to Fairhaven."

"Really?" Her hopes soared. She didn't want him to lose his job, but if it happened, maybe that would be for the best.

But what if his job situation didn't change? What would they do then? Her stomach tensed as that painful possibility rose in her mind. She quickly pushed it away. Why worry about that now? She'd deal with it later if she had to.

"We'll work it out somehow. I promise." He pulled her closer and wrapped his arms around her.

This time she hugged him tight. The plush warmth of his jacket brushed her cheek, and underneath she heard the strong and steady beat of his heart.

Alex trudged through the door of his San Francisco apartment Sunday evening, carrying his computer case and a sack of mail his downstairs neighbor had collected for him while he'd been away. He reached to turn on the lights, and pain shot through his stiff neck and left shoulder. He groaned, tossed the mail onto the kitchen counter and tried to massage away the tightness at the base of his neck.

These past two days had been an agonizing marathon.

Saying goodbye to Annie on Friday night had been more difficult than he'd imagined. Before dawn on Saturday, he caught the train to Seattle, then took the first flight out to San Francisco. Even though he raced from the airport to the office, he'd been twenty minutes late for the noon meeting. His boss had not been happy. But it couldn't be helped.

The merger strategy talks had run until after ten last night and eight tonight, with discussions that pushed him past the edge of frustration. Jobs were being cut with little thought to how the people involved would survive.

He opened the refrigerator and glanced inside. No food had magically appeared since he'd checked this morning. All he had was a wrinkled apple, a small container of blueberry yogurt and a half-empty carton of orange juice that was probably sour by now.

Great. What was he supposed to eat for dinner?

He should've stopped and picked up something on the way home, but he was so exhausted he hadn't even thought about dinner until he walked in the door.

Memories of the delicious meals Annie prepared three times a day flashed through his mind, and he groaned again. Why hadn't he realized how depressing it was cooking for one and living alone in this cold, impersonal apartment?

Grabbing his cell phone, he punched in Annie's number. While he waited for the call to go through, he took a box of cereal from the cabinet and poured some into a bowl.

Annie picked up after the third ring.

He looked into the fridge for milk, then remembered he

didn't have any. He shook his head, grabbed the yogurt and dumped it over his cereal.

"How are you doing?" she asked.

"I'm surviving, but it's been a battle." He gave her a rundown of the plans they'd made to deal with the merger. "How about you?" He took a bite of cereal and yogurt and grimaced. It tasted like mushy cardboard with a little sugar on top.

"We're okay. Emma's tooth came out."

A smile tugged at one side of his mouth. "Wish I could see that."

"Maybe we can take a picture and email it to you."

That didn't ease the ache in his chest, but he didn't want to sound ungrateful. "Thanks."

"I'm planning to put a dollar under her pillow tonight." He heard the smile in her voice.

"She'll like that," he said, fighting off a wave of melancholy.

"She's pretty excited. As soon as her tooth came out, she washed it off, wrapped it in a tissue and stuck it under her pillow."

"Good for her."

"And when she prayed at dinner, she asked God to hurry and send her a new tooth so she wouldn't have to miss too many meals."

He grinned, and the ache in his chest faded a little. "I hope you told her she could still eat."

"Of course, but she had a hard time hearing me because Irene was laughing so hard, tears were rolling down her cheeks."

Alex shook his head, wishing he'd been there to share that meal and see it all firsthand.

"Jason stopped by tonight. Irene signed the contract. He

had another job cancel, so he'll put all his efforts into the bakery."

"I wonder why he lost that other job."

"I don't know, but that means ours should be finished sooner. We might be able to reopen by mid-January."

Alex forced himself to swallow one more bite of soggy cereal, then pushed the bowl away. "Did Gram get him to change that clause on the last page?"

"Yes. He said it wasn't a problem."

"Good." Alex set the bowl in the sink and ran water over it, washing the mushy mess down the drain. "I'll give Jason a call. I want to be sure he knows I'm still involved in the project even though I'm not in town."

"That's a good idea. It should help keep him accountable."

"Right."

"So what about your job, Alex? Do you have any clear sense about what's going to happen?"

He crossed the living room and sank onto one end of the couch. "My boss is going to push to keep me on, but there's no way of knowing for sure until later this week."

She released a soft sigh.

He closed his eyes, missing Annie more than he thought possible. Everything in him longed to hold her and reassure her it would all work out. But how could he do that when he had no idea what was going to happen?

"If it was just my job, it wouldn't be so bad, but we're trying to figure out a way to save jobs for seventy-three people. A lot of them are married, and they have kids. They need their health insurance." He rubbed his forehead. "I'm so tired of dealing with all this corporate wrangling."

"I'm sorry, Alex." Compassion filled her voice.

"Honestly, Annie, if they let me go, it would almost be a relief." He glanced around his apartment and shook his head. Why had he been in such a hurry to get back to San Francisco? The life he had here was not nearly as meaningful as what he could have in Fairhaven with Annie.

"I'm praying for you, Alex. I know this is hard."

His eyes burned. He closed them and laid his head back on the couch cushions.

"Selfishly, I want you to come back here and run the bakery with me, but I'm trusting God to work out what's best for you and for us."

His throat tightened, and he had to force out his words. "Thanks, Annie. I'm praying, too."

"Then we'll be okay," she said softly.

"Yeah, I'm sure we will," He willed confidence into his voice for Annie's sake. He didn't want her to worry, but he still couldn't see a clear path for the future. Only one thing was sure: no matter what happened with his job, he had to figure out a way for them to be together. Because being apart from Annie didn't make sense anymore.

Chapter Fifteen

Annie scooted the last box of Christmas decorations toward the opening in the attic floor. She'd already carried five other totes and boxes down for Irene. But as they worked on decorating the house, Irene had realized the olive-wood nativity she'd purchased in Israel almost forty years ago was still in the attic, so she'd sent Annie back to search for one last box.

The beam of Annie's flashlight illuminated a box sitting nearby. Alex's name was written on the side. Memories of the last time she'd been in the attic with Alex tugged at her heart.

She knelt and opened the box. Alex's Bible lay on top of the pile of clothes. She ran her hand over the soft brown leather and lifted it from the box. Closing her eyes, she held it close to her heart.

Her nightly phone conversations with Alex rose in her mind. The merger had been announced three days ago, and his job was still hanging in the balance. He needed the wisdom recorded in these pages now more than ever. But the good news was that his heart had slowly been opening to the Lord.

Maybe she should mail him the Bible so he'd have it there in San Francisco. Or perhaps she'd put it on the nightstand in his room with the hope that he'd come back soon.

A bittersweet pang shot through her heart. Would he come home for Christmas? Would he be here to bake cookies with them, fill Emma's stocking and attend the Christmas Eve service? He was already missing decorating the house, though the Christmas tree they'd cut down last Friday still sat out back, resting against the house with its stump in a bucket of water. She couldn't quite convince herself to bring the spruce in and decorate it without Alex.

She placed Alex's Bible on top of the box, then carefully carried them down the ladder. After closing the attic, she walked down the hall and stopped in front of the open door to Alex's room.

His bed was neatly made, but his running shoes and extra computer cord sat on the bench by the closet, along with a stack of clean clothes she'd lovingly washed, folded and placed there for him, waiting for his return.

Her heart clenched. He'd been gone only six days, and already she missed him so much she could hardly breathe when she thought of him being so far away.

When would she see him again? New Year's? Valentine's Day? Would this time apart cool his affection for her? How long until his nightly phone calls became weekly updates, then stopped altogether?

What if he never came back?

No. She would not let those fears have a place in her heart. She laid the Bible on his nightstand, sank onto the edge of his bed and lowered her head. *Father, please help me have faith in Your plan and in Alex and the promises he's made. Please give me strength to believe the best about Alex. Give our love a chance to grow, for all our sakes.*

She was just about to whisper "amen" when Irene called her name from downstairs.

"Did you find that box?"

Annie rose from the bed. "Yes, I've got it. I'll be down

in a minute." She turned and smoothed the wrinkles out of Alex's bedspread. If only she could smooth out the wrinkles in her life as easily. With one last glance at the Bible on the nightstand, she turned and walked out of his room, her heart still playing a game of tug-of-war between hope and doubt.

Thirty minutes later, Irene sank into her recliner with a satisfied sigh. "My goodness, I didn't realize how many decorations I've collected over the years."

Annie looked around with a smile. Little white lights twinkled in the evergreen and holly branches they'd laid across the mantel. Irene's angel collection filled the top of the dining-room buffet, and three unique nativity sets held places of honor in the living room. "The house looks beautiful, Irene."

"Thank you, dear. I never could've done it without you."

"I'm glad to help." Annie glanced at Emma. She lay on the living-room rug, wearing a red plush Santa hat and playing with a child's plastic nativity set, lost in her own world.

Irene nodded toward Emma. "It's good to see a child playing with that set again. Leslie bought it for Alex and Steven when they were boys."

Annie sat at the end of the couch closest to Irene. "Leslie was Alex's mother?"

"Yes. She and my son, David, were wonderful parents. They made sure the boys knew the true meaning of Christmas." Irene pressed her lips together, and tears glistened in her eyes. "Even though it's been sixteen years, it's still hard to believe they're gone."

Annie reached over and squeezed her hand. "I'm sorry, Irene. I can't imagine how hard it would be to lose your son, daughter-in-law and a grandson all at once like that."

"Thank you, dear. You're very sweet." She sniffed and reached for a tissue. "I'm not sure how we made it through that time. But we had to take care of Alex. I suppose that's what kept us going."

"He's only mentioned it to me once. I could tell it's hard for him to talk about it." She hesitated, then lifted her gaze to meet Irene's. "If it's not too painful for you, I'd like to know what happened."

Irene clutched the tissue. "Yes, you should know so you can understand Alex better."

Her gaze drifted to the front window. "They were on vacation in northern California, camped in the forest by a small stream. One evening there was a heavy storm, and it turned that little stream into a raging torrent. A flash flood swept through their campground. Alex grabbed hold of a tree and screamed for help. His father tried to reach him, but he was swept away while Alex watched." Irene dabbed her eyes again. "Such a tragedy, and such a burden for Alex to carry."

A dreadful shiver raced up Annie's back, and she swallowed. "What about his mother and brother? Did he see…" But she couldn't finish her question.

"No, he never saw what happened to them. God spared him from that."

"I'm so sorry," Annie whispered.

"It was very difficult for Alex. He was only twelve at the time."

Annie nodded, trying to absorb the story. Her father had left her mother when she was young, but at least she heard from him once or twice a year on her birthday or Christmas.

"I've often wondered if losing his parents and brother is the reason he's been so focused on his career rather than settling down and starting a family."

Annie tipped her head. "You'd think losing them would make him want a family more than ever."

"I believe down deep he wants a family." She shook her

head sadly. "But I'm afraid the possibility of losing someone he loves has made him hesitant to commit to a relationship. In Alex's eyes, the risks are too great, and it's safer to pour himself into his job."

Annie sat back, considering Irene's words. Had Alex returned to San Francisco to distance himself from her and short-circuit their relationship?

Irene reached for her hand. "But don't worry, dear. I've been praying about this for a long time, and I believe the Lord is finally answering my prayer by bringing you here."

"Really?"

Irene nodded. "Alex needs to work through these issues, and I think you might be just the woman to help him do it."

Annie let that thought settle in her heart. Could she help Alex put his painful past to rest? She certainly could relate to the losses and feelings of anger and rejection that went along with them. She'd struggled with those very issues for a long time. Only in the past couple years had she allowed the Lord to comfort her and begin to heal those wounds. If she shared what she'd learned with Alex, would it help him find the healing he needed?

But putting her heart on the line for a man who didn't have a history of commitment was a risk—a huge risk.

She settled back on the couch, pondering all that Irene had told her. If she truly loved Alex, then she should be willing to do whatever she could to help him, even face the possibility of a broken heart.

Emma hopped up and joined her on the couch. "Can we put up the lights now?"

Annie blinked and turned to her daughter. "What?"

"You said we could put lights around the window." Emma pointed to the two strings of Christmas lights that lay on the floor by the couch.

Annie brushed the curls back from her daughter's face, thankfulness filling her heart. "Sure, let's put up those lights."

Alex looked out the side passenger window of the cab as it turned down his grandmother's street. The wet pavement glistened in the reflective glow of the streetlights. Raindrops splashed against the window, blurring his view of the Christmas lights the neighbors had strung across their rooflines, porches and yards.

"It's the fourth house on the right."

"Okay." The cabdriver slowed and pulled into the driveway. He looked over his shoulder. "Bet you're glad to get home before this rain turns into sleet or snow."

"Very glad." Alex grabbed his computer bag from the seat and climbed out of the cab. He'd prayed the storm wouldn't delay his flight or strangle traffic between the train station and his grandmother's home, and his prayers had been answered.

The driver lifted Alex's suitcase from the trunk and extended the handle. Alex handed the man two twenties. "Keep the change."

"Thanks." The driver tapped the bill of his Seattle Seahawks cap in a jaunty salute and hustled off.

Alex gazed up at Irene's house. Golden light glowed in the windows, sending out a warm welcome. He towed his bag across the stone walkway, torn between running up the stairs to see Annie and hanging out on the porch for a few minutes to figure out what he was going to say to her.

He hadn't told her he was coming home, even though they'd talked on the phone last night. He'd told himself he wanted to surprise her, but the truth was he didn't quite know how to explain they'd let him go.

What would she think of him now? And how could they make plans for the future when he didn't have a job?

A silhouette rose in the front window, and then a string of white lights flashed on, revealing Annie's face and lovely form.

His breath snagged in his throat, and his hesitation faded. Coming home to Annie was definitely better than sitting alone in his San Francisco apartment trying to figure out what came next. There was nothing to hold him in San Francisco now, and there were so many reasons to come home.

He carried his suitcase up the steps, pushed open the front door and strode into the living room.

Annie plugged in the string of lights and stepped up on the chair. If she strung the lights over the end of the curtain rod and wrapped them around again in the middle, maybe she could make this work.

"Be careful, dear. I don't want you to break your neck," Irene called from her recliner. "Do you want me to come help you?"

"No, I'm fine. I'll get it." She rose on her tiptoes, straining to reach the rod. If only she were a little taller.

The front door opened, and Alex walked into the living room. Annie gasped and teetered toward the edge of the chair.

"Whoa!" Alex rushed forward and steadied her with a firm grasp around her waist.

Annie blinked as the warmth of his hands traveled through her, heating her all the way to her toes.

"Alex!" Emma ran to him and wrapped her arms around his legs.

"For goodness' sakes," Irene said. "You're going to give me another heart attack, surprising us like that."

"Sorry, Gram." He took Annie's hand and helped her down from the chair.

Annie could barely find her voice. "What are you doing here?"

He grinned. "I was hoping for a little more of an enthusiastic greeting than that."

"Sorry." She hugged him, closing her eyes and taking another moment to let the wonderful surprise sink in. Finally she stepped back.

Emma tugged on his pants leg. "Do you want to see where I lost my tooth?" Without waiting for his reply, she opened her mouth and pointed to the empty spot.

He leaned down and tipped up her chin. "Well, look at that." He narrowed his eyes. "I can see all the way to your tonsils."

Emma's mouth snapped closed. "My what?"

"He's teasing you, sweetie."

"Oh…well, the Tooth Fairy left me a whole dollar." She smiled at Annie, looking as if they shared a delightful secret.

"That's great." He gave her a gentle pat on the head. He took off his jacket and walked over to the front closet.

Annie followed him. "I'm glad you're here, but I don't understand. When we talked last night, you didn't say anything about coming home."

"Things have changed. And I thought it would be best if I explained them in person."

Annie read the truth in his eyes. He'd lost his job. That had to be a terrible blow. But like the fog slowly lifting, another truth became clear. If he was no longer tied to his job in San Francisco, he was free to stay in Fairhaven. He could oversee the renovations, be here to help with the transition as they reopened, and maybe…just maybe he'd stay and partner with her to manage the new Jameson's Bakery Café. A surge of hopefulness flooded her heart.

"Let's sit down." He took her hand and led her back to the couch. After they settled in, he poured out the story.

"So they let you go after all the hard work you've put in the last seven years?" Irene glared toward the fireplace. "Ungrateful tyrants."

"It's business, Gram. The guy who runs marketing for Wyndham is related to the CEO. Once I heard that, I knew the chances of them keeping me on were slim."

Irene huffed. "Well, you deserve better treatment than that."

"Maybe." He looked off toward the window and rubbed his chin. "But they can't keep people on the payroll they don't need."

"They'll be sorry they let you go."

"Thanks, Gram." Alex shifted his gaze to Annie. "My lease is up at the end of the month, so I packed up yesterday and turned in the key."

She pulled in a quick breath. "You moved out of your apartment?"

He nodded. "I gave away some furniture to friends and put the rest in storage. I'm not really a collector. I don't have too much there."

Irene pushed down the footrest of her recliner. "I'm sorry about your job, but I'm thrilled to have you home for Christmas."

Alex shifted his gaze to Annie. "Me, too."

Her heart stirred and lifted. Having Alex home for Christmas would be wonderful, and it was only the beginning for them.

Chapter Sixteen

Alex took Annie's hand as they rounded the corner and walked toward the bakery. Even through his black leather gloves, he could feel the comforting warmth of her hand in his. He might not know exactly what lay ahead, but he was sure of one thing—coming home to Fairhaven was the right decision. With Annie by his side, he could meet whatever challenges came his way.

"Oh, look, they're putting up the sign." Annie clasped his hand more tightly, and they quickened their pace.

Scaffolding had been set up across the front of the building. Two men worked up top, attaching the sign above the doorway. But that wasn't the only change Alex noticed.

The bricks had been steam cleaned, brightening their deep red color. The trim was painted warm gold and rich terra-cotta. New awnings with bold black-and-white stripes and a scalloped edge hung above the front window and door.

"I can't believe they've made so much progress in just a week."

Annie smiled and nodded. "Wait until you hear the story about the awnings."

"What about them?"

"They were intended for another job, but the company

sent a double order by mistake. And they just happened to be the size we needed, so Jason was able to give them to us at a great price."

"Makes you think someone up there likes us."

She squeezed his hand. "I know He does."

He scanned the front of the building again, trying to imagine how the bakery would look when the scaffolding was removed. "The awnings will give us some nice shade. Maybe we could offer outdoor seating when the weather warms up."

Her eyes glowed as she looked up at him. "I was thinking the same thing."

"Well, you know what they say. Great minds think alike."

She laughed softly. "Right."

"How's the progress coming inside?"

"They just started in there a couple days ago."

"Let's take a look." He held open the door for her, then followed her in.

Plastic sheeting hung over the opening to the kitchen, but the rest of the room was mostly empty. The old bakery case and counters had been removed, leaving a large open area.

Jason pushed aside the sheeting and stepped through from the kitchen. "Hey, Alex, I didn't expect to see you here." He sent a questioning glance at Annie. His gaze dropped to their clasped hands. An undefined emotion flashed across his face, then disappeared just as quickly.

Alex held tight to Annie's hand. It was time Jason knew he and Annie were more than friends.

"Things are looking good out front," Alex said, glancing over his shoulder.

"I'm glad we didn't get that snow they were predicting. I wanted to get that sign up today."

"I told Alex about the awnings," Annie said.

"Yeah, that saved us some time and money."

Alex nodded and looked around. "So what's next?"

Jason motioned toward the east wall. "We're just about done tearing things out in here." He went on to explain the demolition work they'd done in the kitchen, looking pleased with the progress.

Alex nodded. Even though he'd been hesitant to hire Jason, he seemed to be doing a good job. "So when do you think we can reopen?"

"January 15 is my target date, but that depends on when the new kitchen equipment arrives. I can keep my guys busy working on the floor and walls, but we've got to have that equipment to get the kitchen finished. Give me another week or two, and I'll be able to give you a firm date."

Alex glanced around once more. "Okay. We appreciate what you're doing."

"Thanks. I don't think we'll have any trouble finishing up on time." He shifted his gaze to Annie and smiled. "I promised Annie I'd give her my best."

Alex slipped his arm around Annie's shoulder. "She definitely deserves that."

"Yes, she does." Jason nodded. "Well, I better get back to work." He reached out and shook hands with Alex, then nodded to Annie. "I'll see you in church on Sunday."

Alex and Annie walked outside and headed back to the car. When they were half a block away, Annie glanced at him. "I've been thinking through some of the details for reopening, and I'm not sure how I'm going to juggle getting Emma off to school and also supervise the morning shift. And what about Irene?"

"I think Gram could manage at home in the morning without you."

"Maybe, but she can't drive herself to therapy or appointments, or carry in groceries or climb stairs."

"I can help her." Alex unlocked the passenger door for

Annie. "And we have at least a month before we open. That gives us time to work it all out."

"True, but I'd like to give Harry and Janelle an idea of their hours." She slid into the car and fastened her belt.

Alex climbed in on his side and started the engine. "Let's look at the calendar when we get home."

She nodded, but slight lines creased her forehead.

He reached over and took her hand. "Don't worry. I'll be here. We can tackle this together."

She leaned over and kissed his cheek. "That's all I need to hear."

Annie sat on the log and bent to unzip her boots. Uncertainty swirled through her stomach as she scanned the frozen pond surrounded by tall, frosty evergreens. "I don't know about this, Alex."

He settled on the log next to her. "Hey, it's going to be fun."

"But I haven't ice-skated since I was Emma's age."

"That just means it's way past time you put on some skates and hit the ice."

"Hitting the ice is exactly what I'm worried about."

He chuckled. "You'll do great. I haven't skated since I was a kid, either, but I was pretty good. I'll help you get started." He pulled on his skates with ease and laced them. "I'm sure once you're on the ice it'll all come back to you."

Maybe he was sure…but she wasn't. The few times she'd tried skating, she'd spent more time clutching the railing around the edge of the rink than gliding across the ice.

If Alex hadn't been so excited today, she wouldn't have agreed to come. The last thing she wanted to do was fall on her face and make a fool of herself in front of him. But there was no way around it now. She'd just have to go out on the ice and give it a try.

She slowly slipped her feet into the skates, wishing she could delay the inevitable.

"Here, let me give you a hand." He knelt in front of her and took over lacing her skates. "You want them to be tight enough to support your ankles, but not too tight to be uncomfortable."

"Thanks." The bright sun shone down on Alex, highlighting the strong contours of his face, his straight nose and square jaw. He was a handsome man, but more than that, he was a kind man and a good man, and every day she became more sure of it.

This past week she and Alex had grown even closer as they cared for Emma and Irene, prepared for Christmas and made plans to reopen the bakery. Everything was so much easier and more enjoyable with Alex around. His organizational skills helped keep them all on schedule, and his sense of humor lightened the mood and brightened her days.

Each evening they spent time playing games, reading aloud with Emma and talking. And when the fire burned low and it was finally time to say good-night, they shared a sweet kiss. He never pushed for more or made her feel uncomfortable. He was a gentleman, and his attention and affection made her feel special and treasured.

Even though he hadn't said he loved her, every day he'd showed her how much he cared, and her heart felt more safe and secure.

Alex tied the last lace and looked up at her. "How does that feel? Too tight?"

"No, it's just right. Thanks." She leaned forward and placed a feathery kiss on his lips.

He looked at her, his blue eyes shining. "I'll have to take you skating more often."

She laughed softly as he pulled her to her feet. "Remember, I have no idea what I'm doing."

"No problem. We'll take it nice and slow."

"Okay."

"The first thing you want to do is step onto the ice sideways."

She held his hand in a death grip and planted her skates on the ice. A cool breeze swept across the surface of the pond and swirled around her legs, making her wish she'd worn another layer beneath her jeans.

"Now make a V with your feet and bend your knees slightly."

She felt totally ridiculous, but she followed his instructions.

"Bending your knees helps keep your weight over your skates so you have more control, and hopefully you won't fall."

"Wonderful." She couldn't keep the sarcasm out of her voice.

"Now raise your hands out to the side, about even with your hips. That'll help you keep your balance."

She clenched her teeth and let go of his hand.

"Good. Now take small steps like this." He showed her what he meant. "You want to get used to the feeling of your skates."

She took a few timid steps, waddling across the ice. "Oh, I must look like a penguin."

He grinned. "Maybe a little. But you're a very cute penguin."

She laughed, relaxing her stance, and as she did, her feet started to slide. She gasped, and her arms shot out to the side.

Alex grabbed her with a firm hand on her waist, the other gripping her hand. "Steady."

Her heartbeat pounded in her ears, and a shiver raced down her arms. "Whoa."

"I've got you. You're not going to fall." He lifted his eyebrow and sent her a cocky grin. "Ready to try again?"

"Do I have to?"

"No, but you'll miss all the fun if you don't."

She released a dramatic sigh. "Okay."

He let go, and she took a few more small steps that ended with short glides. She looked up and sent him a tentative smile.

"Very nice. Let's try pushing off with one foot." He demonstrated the moves with an easy grace that made it look effortless.

"Where did you learn to skate like that?"

"I played hockey for a while before I tried out for basketball."

"I didn't know that."

He skated around her in a circle, stopping in front of her with a flourish. "There are a lot of things you don't know about me."

She returned his teasing smile. "Is that right?"

"Yep." He skated around her again, coming closer.

"I'm looking forward to learning more."

He placed his arm around her waist, and they set off across the pond. With the comfort and safety of his arm around her, she relaxed and found herself matching his smooth strokes. Soon they gained speed and were gliding at a faster pace. The brisk breeze made her nose and cheeks tingle. "Maybe we should slow down."

He grinned. "Don't worry, you're safe with me." But two seconds later his skate hit a rough patch, and the jolt threw him off balance.

He let go of Annie, and she sailed off across the pond, her arms flailing as she pitched forward and back, trying to stay upright. "Alex!"

She heard him skating up behind her, but she couldn't turn, and she didn't know how to stop.

He grabbed her arm, trying to slow her crazy dance. "Hold on!"

She twisted toward him. Her legs shot out from under her, and they both went down in a wild tangle of arms and legs.

Alex hit the ice first, then Annie landed on top of him, and the air whooshed out of his lungs. His body softened her fall, but her left knee crashed onto the ice. Pain shot up her leg like a burning arrow.

Stunned, she lay there panting for a second, then opened her eyes and blinked at Alex.

He lay face up on the ice, eyes closed, as still as a dead man.

Her heart jerked in her chest. "Alex?" She shoved herself onto her knees and shook his shoulder. "Alex!"

He slowly opened his eyes and stared at her. "What happened?"

"We crashed. Are you okay?"

He blinked a couple times. "Who are you?"

Alarm shot through her. "What?" She stared at him a second. Surely he was joking. "Stop it, Alex. That's not funny."

He narrowed his eyes. "Why are you calling me Alex?"

"Because that's your name!" She sat back on her heels, her mind spinning. She searched across the pond. Her phone was in her backpack, by the log where they'd put on their skates. How was she going to get over there?

A smile trembled at the corners of his mouth, and he finally broke out laughing. "I'm okay, Annie."

She gasped. "Oh, you're terrible." Glaring at him, she gave his shoulder a playful shove. But it was hard to stay mad when his eyes twinkled with humor and his laughter was so full and free.

"I'm sorry," he said when he finally caught his breath.

"But you're so much fun to tease." He sat up, shook the ice off his gloves and watched her with a playful smile.

His knit hat had slipped a few inches to the side. She reached up and tugged it back in place. "You shouldn't scare me like that. I was about to crawl across the pond to get my phone and call 9-1-1."

He captured her hand and pulled her closer. The teasing look in his eyes mellowed. "You'd do that? You'd crawl across the pond?"

"Of course. If you needed help I'd crawl back to town."

"I believe you would." He kissed her then, melting her heart and leaving her breathless.

Chapter Seventeen

Annie hummed "I'm Dreaming of a White Christmas" as she stood in front of the dryer and shook out Alex's long-sleeved T-shirt. The soft warmth of the cotton fabric sent a comforting wave through her. She folded it and placed it on top of the pile in the laundry basket. Alex had worn that shirt yesterday when he'd taken her skating.

Alex's kiss replayed in her mind. The tender look in his eyes and sweetness of that moment sent a melting sensation through her again.

She'd never felt like this before, not with Kevin or anyone else. No man had ever captured her heart this way and made her feel so special.

With a soft sigh, she scooped up the laundry basket and carried it into the kitchen.

Irene stood at the counter consulting a cookbook. She looked up and smiled at Annie. "I thought I'd try my hand at this recipe for oven-barbecued chicken."

Annie set the basket on the table and joined Irene. "That sounds good." She scanned the nutrition facts at the bottom of the recipe.

"Don't worry. It's healthy."

Annie patted her back. "I'm proud of you, Irene."

"You mean for finally getting up out of my recliner?"

"No, I'm proud of you for taking charge of your health and being willing to try new things."

"Well, it's high time I got back in the kitchen." She pulled an apron from the drawer. "Not that I haven't enjoyed your cooking. It's been wonderful, but I'm feeling stronger, and I want to do my part. Besides, you'll be managing the bakery soon. You won't have time to fuss over me."

Annie smiled. "I've loved living here and cooking for you. You've been so kind to me and tolerant of Emma. I know it hasn't been easy having a five-year-old underfoot all the time."

"Underfoot? Nonsense. I've loved every minute of it. I'm sure that's one reason I've recovered so quickly."

"That's sweet of you to say."

Irene reached for Annie's hand. "I want you to know how grateful I am. I don't know what I would've done without your help."

Annie's throat tightened, and she hugged Irene. "Staying here with you has been a blessing for me and Emma."

Irene stepped back, all misty-eyed. "Look at us—a couple of blubbery women."

Annie laughed and wiped a tear from the corner of her eye. "We've been happy here. You've treated us like family. That's a priceless gift."

Irene's eyes sparkled. "Well, you are family to me. And if I'm reading my grandson right, maybe you'll become family in a more permanent way very soon."

Annie blushed and looked away, but she held that same hope in her heart. "I better put away this laundry. I have to go pick up Emma soon."

"All right, dear." Irene sent her a smile.

Annie picked up the laundry basket, humming her Christmas carol again, and carried it upstairs.

* * *

Alex's phone rang. He picked it up from the desk in his bedroom and glanced at the screen. Why was Tiffany Charles calling him?

"Hey, Alex, it's good to hear your voice. How are you doing?"

"I'm okay."

"I got a call from Steve this morning. He says Hyatt is looking for a new sales-and-marketing manager for their Midwest region."

His pulse jumped, and he straightened. "I've heard good things about Hyatt. Are you going to apply?"

"Me? No. I can't move to Chicago in the middle of the school year. And trying to sell my house in this market would be a nightmare. But you could go. You're a free man."

He paced across the room. "I don't know. I've got some opportunities here I'm working on right now."

"Really? In Fairhaven? I thought you said they didn't have many hotels up there."

"We have a few." He didn't want to tell her his opportunity was working for his grandmother in the family bakery. She wouldn't understand, and it was none of her business anyway. He pushed his discomfort aside. "What else did Steve say about the job?"

Tiffany listed the facts, and each one made the job sound more appealing.

"I think you should go for it, Alex. It sounds like a great opportunity for you."

Conflicting thoughts raced through his mind. Did he really want to stay in Fairhaven and reopen the bakery when there was a chance he could work for Hyatt and move ahead in his career? But would Annie want to live in Chicago? And who would manage the bakery if he took a job and she followed him out there? What about his grandmother? Who would watch out for her?

"Opportunities like this don't come around every day," Tiffany continued. "I'm sure they're going to offer a good salary and benefits. You should jump on it before word gets out."

Questions and doubts battled in his mind, but he closed his eyes and pushed them aside. He'd deal with them later. Right now he needed to get all the information he could from Tiffany. "Does Steve have a contact at Hyatt? Did he give you any names?"

"Yeah, he gave me two."

"Great. Let me get a pen." He walked over to the desk and jotted the information on the back of an envelope.

"I'm glad you're going to follow up on this. I'd hate to think of you stuck up there in that small town with all your skills and talents going to waste."

"Thanks, Tiff. I appreciate the call. This could be a good career move for me. I'll check it out."

Annie sagged against the wall outside Alex's room as he continued his conversation with Tiffany. Hot tears burned her eyes.

What a fool she'd been, thinking Alex would want to stay in Fairhaven and run the bakery with her. He'd worked in marketing for years, managing a team of people at a big company. He'd never be happy working for his grandmother, serving soup and sandwiches to folks in his hometown.

She thought his attention and affection meant he planned to settle down and build a future with her. She'd spun a beautiful dream and convinced herself it was true.

But she was wrong.

He'd never promised to stay.

He didn't love her…at least not enough to marry her and make Fairhaven his home.

Alex chuckled at something Tiffany said. Annie leaned forward. A slight wave of guilt hit her heart. She shouldn't be listening at his door, but hadn't she prayed to know the truth? Hadn't she asked God to keep her from going down the wrong path and giving her heart away if Alex wasn't the right man for her?

Was this God's answer to her prayer? Was he warning her to stay away from Alex and save herself from more heartache?

A painful lump lodged in her throat. She placed the basket of clean clothes on the floor by his door and turned away. Her heart felt like a stone in her chest as she trudged down the stairs, away from Alex. His voice grew distant, and her tears overflowed.

What a fool. The words played over and over in her head. She'd opened her heart and been betrayed again.

When would she finally accept the truth? No man would ever love her enough to stick around and keep his promises.

Alex heard a soft thump in the hallway. He frowned and glanced over his shoulder. Annie and his grandmother were both home, but Gram wasn't supposed to be climbing the stairs. He ended the call with Tiffany, crossed the room and looked out the door. The hallway was empty, except for a basket of clean clothes.

A flash of concern rose and tightened his chest. Had Annie overheard that phone call?

No, if she had, she would've come in and asked him about it. Still, the thought of talking to her about the possible job in Chicago made his stomach tighten.

It would be best if he waited until he had all the facts before he had that conversation. Maybe the position would already be filled, and he wouldn't have to say anything. Why upset her for no good reason?

* * *

Alex glanced across the dining-room table at Annie, and his spirit deflated. She'd hardly touched her food, and she'd avoided looking at him all through dinner. If Emma hadn't kept the conversation going with her constant chatter, he doubted Annie would've spoken a word to any of them.

Something was definitely wrong, and he wasn't the only one who noticed. Gram's anxious gaze darted from Annie to him. She tipped her head toward Annie and sent him a pointed look.

He lifted his shoulder in a slight shrug. But the possibility that she'd overheard the phone call was the only reason he could come up with to explain her mood. That thought made the food in his stomach congeal like a lump of clay.

"Well, that was a lovely dinner, if I do say so myself." Gram laid her napkin on the table.

Annie looked up and blinked. "The chicken was delicious."

"It doesn't look like you ate enough to know how it tasted." Gram's concerned gaze swept over Annie. "You're awfully pale, dear. Are you feeling all right?"

"I'm fine. I'm just not very hungry tonight." Annie laid her fork across her plate.

"All right, then." Gram pushed her chair back. "I have a Christmas project I'm working on in my room, and I could use some help from a certain young lady who's very good at cutting and taping." She smiled at Emma.

Emma's eyes lit up. "I can help you."

"Would you, dear? That would be wonderful." Gram stood. "Alex, would you help Annie with the dishes so Emma and I can get started right away?"

"Sure. I'd be glad to."

"That's not necessary. I'll take care of it." Annie got up and reached for the platter of chicken.

Alex grabbed the other side and held on. "No. I insist."

Their gazes locked over the table. Emotion flashed in her eyes, and she dropped hold of the platter. "Fine."

Alex followed her into the kitchen and set the platter on the counter. "I know you're upset. Do you want to tell me what's wrong?"

"Nothing's wrong." She sprayed water over a plate and shoved it in the dishwasher.

Obviously that wasn't true. He stepped up behind her and placed his hand on her shoulder.

She flinched and pulled away. "Don't touch me."

He froze. "What?"

She turned and faced him, her dark eyes burning like molten lava. "You heard what I said."

"Yeah, but it doesn't make much sense."

"It does if you're leaving."

Heat flashed up his neck and into his face. He squared his shoulders. "So that's what this is about. You listened in on my phone conversation."

She bristled. "It seems like that's the only way I'm going to find out what's really going on."

"That's not true."

"Why do I find that hard to believe?"

"Because you're upset and blowing this out of proportion."

The color drained from her face. "You said you wanted a relationship with me. You convinced me you cared about us. And all the time you were making plans to leave as soon as you got another job offer." She pulled in a shuddering breath. "When were you going to tell me you're moving to Chicago?"

"Wait a minute, Annie—"

"Why? Why should I wait around for you to lie to me again?"

Fire flashed through him. "I never lied to you. I didn't

say anything about Chicago because I wanted to get all the facts first."

Disbelief hardened her expression.

"I'm telling you the truth. This is not a done deal. It's just a possibility."

"And what if they offer you the job? Are you going to take it? What about the bakery? How am I supposed to manage it by myself?"

He lifted his hands. "I never promised I'd stay in Fairhaven and manage the bakery with you."

"But that's what we talked about. That's what I thought you wanted." A sob cut off her words, and her face crumpled.

"Annie, please don't cry." He couldn't take that.

"I'm not crying." She swiped a tear from the corner of her eye.

"Look, I'm sorry. I didn't know this job with Hyatt was going to come up so soon. I thought we'd have time to launch the bakery and figure things out before I had to make a decision."

"A decision?" Her eyes widened.

"Yes. I have to decide what I'm going to do with the rest of my life, and a big part of that is where I want to live and what I want to do."

"Where *you* want to live…what *you* want to do? That's really what's most important to you?"

"I didn't say that."

Annie shook her head, disbelief in her eyes. "I thought you'd finally figured out that people and relationships are more important than where you work or live. But I guess I was wrong about that. I guess I was wrong about a lot of things." She turned away and started vigorously scrubbing a pot.

"Annie, if you'd just calm down, we could talk about this like reasonable adults."

She gasped and threw the scrubber in the sink. Hot water splashed them both. She spun around, and fire flashed in her eyes. "No! I'm done talking to you about this or anything else." She ran out of the kitchen, and two seconds later her bedroom door slammed so hard it shook the house.

He stared after her, his heart pounding out a painful staccato beat.

Chapter Eighteen

A driving rain lashed Alex's bedroom window early Tuesday morning as he slipped on his suit jacket and turned to face the full-length mirror. Wearing his suit for the flight to Chicago might not be such a good idea, especially in this stormy weather, but the only other choice was cramming it in his carry-on. And that didn't make sense. He had to go straight from the airport to the Hyatt corporate offices for his two-o'clock interview.

A knock sounded at his closed bedroom door.

His pulse jumped. Was it Annie? Had she finally decided to talk to him before he left? "Come in," he called.

The door opened and his grandmother stepped in, wearing her blue bathrobe and a worried frown.

Alex pulled in a sharp breath. "Gram, you're not supposed to climb those stairs."

"I know, but I had to talk to you."

He turned back to the mirror, guilt pressing down on his heart.

Gram walked over and brushed her hand across his shoulder. She looked into the mirror and caught his gaze reflected there. "Are you sure about this, Alex?"

He clenched his jaw and released it. "No, I'm not sure.

But the only way I'm going to find out is to go to Chicago for this interview."

"But what about Annie?"

The ache in his chest deepened. "What about her?"

"She's obviously upset. I'm sure she doesn't want you to go. Can't you talk to her?"

"I've tried, Gram. It doesn't help."

She sank down on the edge of his bed, her rounded shoulders sagging. She looked up at him with a pale, weary expression. She hadn't looked this bad since he'd brought her home from the hospital.

A painful shaft of guilt cut through his heart. He knelt in front of her and took her hand. "Please, Gram, don't worry. It's just an interview. I haven't made up my mind yet."

"But once they talk to you, I know they'll hire you. They'd be crazy not to."

Emotion tightened his throat. "Thanks, Gram. I love you. You've always been there for me."

"I love you, too, and I've always told you the truth." She clasped his hand more tightly. "It's important for a man to have a career and make his way in the world, but that's not the only thing that matters. Love and relationships outweigh that every time. At least they should."

He looked down. "I know, Gram."

"Then why are you walking away from everything and everyone you have here?"

He closed his eyes and pulled in a deep breath. Hadn't he asked himself that same question a thousand times? "This is an important decision, Gram. I have to be sure."

She nodded slowly, then reached out and tenderly touched his cheek. "Well, you have my love, wherever you decide to go, even if it's Chicago."

They both stood, and he hugged her to his chest.

* * *

Raindrops splattered against the glass of Annie's bedroom window as she watched the cab driver load Alex's suitcase into the trunk.

Sheltered by a black umbrella, Alex walked down the porch steps and across the stone walkway toward the cab.

Her vision blurred, and memories carried her back in time. She stood at her childhood bedroom window once more. That day had been sunny, but the same piercing sorrow had cut through her heart as she watched her father climb into his old green truck and drive off, leaving her and her mother behind.

"Where's Alex going?"

Annie blinked and pulled in a quick breath. She hadn't heard Emma walk into the room. "He's going to Chicago on a business trip."

"What kind of business?"

"I don't know."

"When's he coming back?" A hint of fear crept into her daughter's voice, the same fear Annie had felt so long ago.

"I'm not sure." She shivered and wrapped her sweater tighter around herself, but it couldn't protect her from the chill in her heart.

"But he said he would take me to see the Christmas lights."

Annie swallowed. "He said a lot of things."

Emma looked up at Annie with painful questions in her eyes.

Regret tore at Annie's heart. She reached down and scooped up her daughter up for a hug. "I'm sorry, Emma. I'll take you to see the lights."

"But I want to go with Alex."

"I know, sweetie. I know." Annie closed her eyes and hugged her daughter tightly. She wanted that, too, more than she could say, and it made her decision that much harder.

* * *

Irene's eyes grew misty, and she clutched Annie's hand. "But I don't understand. Why would you leave?"

"I'm sorry, Irene. I just think it's best if we do."

"I am getting stronger, but I'm not sure I'm ready to take on everything you've been doing for me, not yet."

"I wouldn't expect you to. I'll come over for a few hours every day to do laundry, cleaning and as much cooking as you'd like. I can drive you to appointments or anywhere you need to go, but I can't stay here any longer."

"But how will you manage? Where will you go?"

"My friend Lilly said we can stay with her." Annie swallowed, not really sure how she would cover all her expenses without the income she'd been earning caring for Irene. Moving again would be difficult, especially for Emma, but she didn't want to be here when Alex returned from Chicago—if he returned.

"What about the bakery?"

"I'll oversee the reopening and stay on until you find someone to replace me, but I can't be your full-time manager." She pressed her lips together to keep from saying, *I'd share that job with Alex if he cared enough about us to stay in Fairhaven.* She didn't want to hurt Irene any more than she already had, so she kept those painful words to herself.

"I wish you'd reconsider. I'm sure the doctor will let me drive soon. I could help take care of Emma and drive her to and from school while you're working at the bakery."

"That's sweet of you, Irene. But I'm afraid managing the bakery on my own would be too much for me to handle."

Irene sank into a chair. "This is because of Alex, isn't it?"

Annie's heart contracted. "What did he say?"

"Nothing! How am I supposed to understand what's going on when neither one of you will tell me?"

"I'm sorry, Irene."

"I'm not trying to be a snoop. You don't have to tell me the details, but can't you just talk to him and work this out? I know he loves you. I'm sure of it."

Annie leaned back against the kitchen counter and shook her head. "Alex doesn't love me, not really. If he did, he'd stay in Fairhaven instead of running off to Chicago for the first job that comes up."

"Going to that interview doesn't change the fact that he loves you."

Annie crossed her arms and stared out the kitchen window. She couldn't let someone who wasn't committed into her heart and life. The cost was too high.

"Honey." Irene walked over and laid her hand on Annie's shoulder. "I know you've been hurt before. You told me about your father leaving when you were a little girl."

Emotion swept through Annie, and her throat burned.

"You never shared the details about Emma's father, but I know he's not involved in your lives, and that has to be painful for you."

She gave a slight nod. She didn't love Kevin, not anymore, but his desertion still hurt.

"I wonder if those painful memories are making it hard for you to see things clearly with Alex."

"What do you mean?"

"Sometimes we bring unresolved hurt from the past into our present relationships, and that distorts things and makes us see everything and everyone through that lens of pain."

Annie thought about that for a moment. "So you think I'm overreacting?"

Irene gave a slight shrug. "Maybe a little."

Annie moaned and rubbed her forehead. "I don't know what to think."

"Why don't you stay and give Alex another chance? He's not perfect, none of us are, but I'm sure he loves you."

"What if he wants to take this job and move to Chicago?"

Irene closed her eyes for a moment, then lifted her gaze to meet Annie's. "If you love him, then maybe you should consider moving there, too."

Annie stared at her. Move to Chicago? Leave Fairhaven and start over in another big, impersonal city with no guarantee that things would work out with Alex? She shook her head, feeling more miserable than ever. "He never told me about Chicago. I overheard it in a phone conversation."

Irene closed her eyes. "Foolish boy," she whispered under her breath. Then she gripped Annie's hand. "When love's at stake, someone has to be the first to show humility and wisdom. Promise me you'll pray on this and ask the Lord to show you what to do."

Annie wrestled with that commitment in her heart, but Irene was right. Praying and waiting for God's direction was much smarter than making a decision based on painful memories or present fears.

She looked at Irene. "All right. I'll pray about it."

Alex stared out the streaked and steamy cab window. Dirty gray snow lined the sidewalks, and bits of trash blew past on icy gusts. People wrapped head to toe in coats, hats, scarves and gloves bent their heads into the wind and trudged through downtown Chicago. No wonder they called it the Windy City.

The cab crawled along at a turtle's pace while horns blared and the song "I Saw Mommy Kissing Santa Claus" poured from the cab's radio speakers.

Alex glanced at his watch, then leaned left and scanned the traffic ahead. "Do you think there's an accident?"

The cabbie looked over his shoulder. "Can't tell. It's like this most days."

"Really?" Alex shifted in his seat and suppressed a groan.

Lack of sleep, a bumpy flight and an empty stomach were doing a number on him. "How long do you think it will take to get to 312 South Wellington?"

"Can't say with this mess in front of us." The cabbie twisted the radio dial, then turned it off with a huff. "I should've listened to my wife and stayed home today." He glanced at Alex in the rearview mirror. "You married?"

Annie's face flashed through his mind, and his stomach clenched. "No."

"Too bad. But you're young. You've got time."

Did he? He was going to turn thirty in February. He'd always thought he'd be married by then. But he hadn't felt ready to make that kind of commitment…until he met Annie.

"You got kids?"

"No, thought I'd wait and find a wife first."

The cabbie chuckled. "Good idea. Me, I've got two kids." He grinned as he flipped down his visor to reveal two pictures. "That's my son, T.J. He's eight. He's a good little soccer player. And that's my daughter, Emily. She's six." He tapped his daughter's photo. "She sings like an angel." He shook his head. "And I promised I'd come to her Christmas program today, but I don't think I'm gonna make it."

Alex frowned. "What time's the program?"

"Two-thirty."

He glanced at his watch. "You've still got forty minutes."

The cabbie shook his head. "I'll never make it unless this traffic gets moving."

Visions of Emma flashed through his mind, her dark eyes sparkling and her happy smile focused on him as she sang at her class Thanksgiving program. Did she have a Christmas program coming up? Would he miss it while he was away on this trip? His chest tightened, and he shifted his gaze to the window.

A tall Christmas tree decorated with hundreds of brightly

colored lights and ornaments came into view in front of the building at the corner. A mother and father approached, holding hands with a little girl about Emma's age. The father lifted her up in his arms so she could have a closer look and touch one of the large ornaments.

Pain seared his heart. He closed his eyes, blocking the poignant image from his view.

"I hate to disappoint my little girl," the cabbie said.

Alex's eyes flew open. Leaning forward, he tapped the back of the cabbie's seat. "Just let me out here. I don't mind walking the rest of the way."

"You kidding? It's at least another mile, and it's freezing out there."

"That's okay."

"Are you sure?"

"Yeah. Go to that program. Be there for your wife and daughter. That's what counts." Alex fished a twenty and a five out of his wallet and passed them to the cabbie. "Keep the change."

"Thanks." He looked back and grinned at Alex. "You're a good man. You saved my neck today."

"No, you saved mine."

Annie sank down in the overstuffed chair and let her gaze travel around the bedroom. Her packed suitcase stood by the door. A cardboard box sat beside it, holding her cookbooks and a few other items she'd collected in the past six weeks. She'd felt so at home here. The possibility of leaving cut a painful swath through her heart.

Maybe she didn't have to go, at least not yet. She'd promised Irene she'd pray about her decision, and she intended to keep that promise.

Closing her eyes, she quieted her thoughts. *Lord, please help me. I don't know what I'm supposed to do. Is Irene right? Have I let the hurts of the past distort what's happening with Alex?*

She sat for a few minutes, waiting until a sense of peace and confirmation settled over her heart.

She needed to let go of the pain from her past and forgive those who had hurt her. Surprise rippled through her. She thought she'd forgiven her father and Kevin—at least she'd voiced those words in prayer.

A portion of a message she'd heard months ago came to mind. The pastor said forgiveness wasn't a onetime event; it was an ongoing process. He compared it to an onion, saying each time another layer was peeled away and painful memories return, we needed to forgive again and release that pain to the Lord. She picked up her Bible and came to a section in Colossians she had underlined sometime in the past. *"Bear with each other and forgive whatever grievances you may have against one another,"* she read. *"Forgive as the Lord forgave you. And over all these virtues put on love, which binds them all together in perfect unity."*

The words seemed to spring off the page and into her heart, and she knew beyond all her doubts what she ought to do.

Annie gripped Emma's hand as they dashed through the rain and into the bakery. The smell of plaster dust and fresh paint greeted Annie as she stepped through the doorway.

Jason stood high up on a ladder in the center of the room, working on a light fixture. He smiled when he saw her, called out a greeting and climbed down. "Crazy weather, isn't it?"

"It sure is." She flicked water off her hands. It dripped on the new beige tile, making little puddles by her feet. "We're going to have to build an ark soon if this rain doesn't stop."

Jason chuckled. "You're right about that."

Annie took a quick survey of the room. "It looks like you're making good progress."

He nodded, looking pleased. "We finished sanding the walls this morning. We're right on schedule."

Annie noticed Jason's daughter sitting at a card table in the corner, coloring. She looked up and smiled at them.

Emma tugged on Annie's hand. "Can I go see Faith?"

Annie hesitated. She only planned to stay for a few minutes, and she didn't want Emma to be upset when they had to leave.

"I hope it's okay that Faith's here." Jason said. "My neighbor usually watches her after school, but her son has the flu, and I didn't want to risk Faith catching it."

"It's fine."

Emma tugged on Annie's hand again. "Can I go see her?"

"Okay, sweetie, just be careful. Don't touch the ladder or any tools."

Emma nodded, then zipped across the room and joined Faith at the table.

"Let me show you why I asked you to come over." He slipped his arm behind her and guided her toward the kitchen.

Annie pulled her damp coat a little tighter around herself, trying to keep her distance without being too obvious.

"The new oven was delivered today," he said, "but it's got a larger door than the old one, so I don't think we should put it in the same place." He showed her how the door swung open. "That would block your pathway between the counter and the mixer."

"Good point." Annie turned and searched the room. "Maybe we should move it over there." They talked for a few minutes, discussing the different options, and finally chose a new location for the oven.

"I'm glad you noticed the problem before you installed it."

He smiled and nodded. "That's my job."

She forced a slight smile in return. "Well, I better get going."

His face fell, and he looked as though he wanted to say something else.

She suspected what it might be, so she hurried on. "Emma and I have some errands we need to run." She turned away, hoping to make her escape.

"Annie, wait a minute."

Her stomach clenched, and she slowly turned to face him. "Yeah?"

"Faith and I are going to see *A Christmas Carol* at Mt. Baker Theater tomorrow night. Would you and Emma like to come with us?"

She didn't want to hurt his feelings, but she needed to be honest. "That's nice of you to ask, but I'm sorry. We can't go."

"Are you sure?" He took a step closer. "It seems like we've got a lot in common. I'd like a chance to get to know you better."

"I'm flattered, Jason, but I'm already seeing someone."

"You mean Alex?"

She nodded.

"But I thought he's taking a job in Chicago."

Her breath caught in her throat. Surely Jason couldn't have heard Alex's decision before she did, could he? No, he was probably just guessing based on hearsay.

"Alex did go there for an interview, but I don't think he's made a decision yet." She pulled in a deep breath, her heart ringing with the truth. "Either way, I'm committed."

Jason nodded. "He's a lucky man." He studied her a moment more. "If you ever change your mind, I hope you'll give me a chance."

Before she answered, the front door opened, and Irene and her Bayside Treasure friends flew in, flapping their umbrellas and squawking like a flock of wet blue jays.

"Oh, I love the new tile." Marian took off her rain hat and shook it out.

Irene set her umbrella by the door. "It's from Italy."

"I hope the rain won't damage it."

"No, I'm sure it's fine. Jason assured me it's totally weatherproof and the perfect color to hide footprints."

Barb strolled across the room. "I can't believe how much more space you have now that they took out the old bakery cases."

Hannah hooked her arm through Irene's. "It's going to be lovely, simply lovely."

Annie smiled at Jason. "Sounds like you've impressed them."

He leaned toward her and lowered his voice. "Wish I could do the same for you."

She shook her head, suppressing a smile. "You don't give up easily, do you?"

"No, but I won't ask you out again unless you let me know you're interested." He motioned toward the front room. "Shall we?"

She nodded and followed him out of the kitchen to greet Irene and her friends.

"I'm glad you're here," Irene said, pulling Annie aside while Jason showed the other women around. "Alex called from the airport in Chicago."

Annie's pulse jumped. "When?"

"About thirty minutes ago. He was just getting on the plane."

Why hadn't he called her? The memory of their last conversation flashed through her mind, providing the answer.

"He said he tried to call you, but you didn't answer."

"He did?" Annie pulled her phone from her purse. Three missed calls from Alex. She groaned. "I must've turned off the ringer and forgot to turn it back on." She flicked the button on the side.

"Don't worry. He should be home around eight tonight."

Annie's stomach fluttered. Alex was coming home.

"Have you made a decision? Are you going to stay?"

Annie nodded and smiled. "I'm staying."

Irene's eyes lit up. "And you'll work things out with Alex?"

"I'll try, if he's willing."

Irene pulled her in for a tight hug. "Oh, I'm so happy."

"Well, Alex might not be. I said some pretty awful things to him before he left."

"I'm sure you can work it out when you talk tonight." She patted Annie's hand. "I won't be there, but I'll pray for you."

"Where are you going?"

"It's Hannah's birthday. The girls and I are taking her out to dinner."

A slight wave of uneasiness rippled through Annie. She took Irene's hand. "I'm glad you're spending time with your friends, but I hope you won't overdo it or stay out too late."

Irene chuckled. "You sound a little like a mother hen, dear."

"Sorry, but you've been doing so well. I don't want you to have a setback."

"Don't worry. I'll be fine." She must've read the concern on Annie's face because she added, "I was just teasing about you being a mother hen. I appreciate you watching out for me." She hugged Annie. "Now, why don't you go home and bake Alex something delicious? Then light a fire in the fireplace and turn on the Christmas lights. You might even play some romantic music."

Annie chuckled. "You want me to set the mood?"

"Yes, that's exactly what I had in mind."

"Why, Irene, you're quite the romantic."

Irene patted her cheek. "You bet I am, honey."

Annie walked over and laid her hand on her daughter's shoulder. "Come on, Emma. It's time to go."

She looked up from her coloring project. "Do we have to?"

"Yes. We've got a party to plan."

Emma's eyes widened. "A party?"

"That's right. A welcome-home party for Alex."

Emma jumped up. "Yippee!"

Chapter Nineteen

Rain pounded the roof of the cab like a drummer beating a frantic rhythm. Alex gripped the handle of his computer case and peered out the cab's streaming windshield. He was certain the driver couldn't see more than a few yards ahead, even though he'd turned the wipers on high.

Alex was sick of riding in cabs and fighting his way through storms. But he was almost home. In a few minutes he'd see Annie and take her in his arms again.

Up ahead, orange cones and police barricades blocked the road.

"What's going on?" Alex leaned forward in the backseat, glaring at the roadblock.

"Looks like Harris is closed off. Maybe there's flooding."

"Cut across Fourteenth. Take McKenzie." Alex clenched his jaw and shifted in his seat. Nothing was going to stop him from getting home. He'd get there if he had to swim.

The cab crawled ahead through the streaming water. Five minutes later they pulled into his grandmother's neighborhood, and he blew out a deep breath.

As they turned the corner, the flashing lights of an ambulance sliced through the darkness.

Alex's heart jerked. The ambulance was parked in his grandmother's driveway.

He yanked off his seat belt. "Hurry! That's my house." He grabbed some bills from his wallet and threw them on the seat. The driver pulled toward the curb, and Alex jumped out. He ran across the muddy lawn and dashed up the steps.

"Hey, what about your suitcase?" the driver called.

Ignoring the driver, he jerked open the door. "Annie?"

She rushed toward him. "Alex!"

Looking past her, he saw three EMTs gathered in the living room. Gram lay on a rolling gurney under a gray blanket. Emma stood frozen by Gram's recliner, her hands clasped in front of her mouth.

"What happened?" Alex dropped his computer case to the floor.

"She went out to dinner with the Treasures, but she started having chest pains."

Alex's heart lurched. "Is it another heart attack?"

"I don't know." Annie's worried gaze focused on Gram. "Marian wanted to take her to the E.R., but she insisted on coming home." Annie turned back to him. "I wasn't sure what to do, but she didn't look good and she was still in pain, so I called 9-1-1."

"Good decision." He ran his hand gently down her arm. "I'm sorry I wasn't here."

"You're here now. That's what counts."

He gave her a quick hug, then stepped forward as the EMTs rolled the gurney toward the front door. "Gram, can you hear me?"

She nodded, and her eyes filled with tears, but she couldn't speak past the oxygen mask covering her mouth.

"Everything's going to be okay." He leaned down and kissed her forehead. "We'll follow you to the hospital."

Annie touched Gram's shoulder. "We love you. We'll be praying."

Gram nodded again, and they whisked her out the door.

Alex followed them out to the porch and grabbed his suitcase the cab driver had left there. Annie and Emma joined him, and they watched the EMTs load the gurney into the back of the ambulance.

"Grab your coats. Let's go." Alex stowed his suitcase inside.

"What about Emma?"

The little girl gripped her mother's hand, her eyes wide. "I want to go with you."

"I know you do, sweetie, but we don't know how long we'll have to stay at the hospital." Annie took her phone from her pants pocket. "Maybe she could stay with Lilly."

"Let's call her on the way." He and Annie quickly gathered a few items for Emma and Irene, then hurried out to Annie's car. Alex climbed into the driver's seat while Annie helped Emma and stowed their bags in the back.

The rain had slowed to a misty drizzle, but water rushed down the edges of the street and overflowed the curbs.

"Harris is closed by Twelfth. We'll have to cut around." Alex backed out of the driveway and headed down the street.

Annie tapped in Lilly's number. A few seconds later she shook her head. "Lilly's not answering. I suppose I could try Jason. His daughter and Emma are friends." But Jason didn't answer, either.

"I think she should come with us," Alex said.

Annie looked over her shoulder and back at him. "But we don't know what's going to happen."

"You're right, but keeping her with us is probably the most reassuring thing we can do."

Annie hesitated a second. "All right."

"I can always bring you both home if we need to." Alex

entered the Five Freeway and headed north toward St. Joseph's Medical Center, pushing the speed limit.

Annie gripped the armrest, but she didn't tell him to slow down.

A few minutes later they took the exit for Sunset Drive, heading west. But as he prepared to turn right on Ellis, roadblocks once again cut off his path. Alex released a frustrated breath. "Great."

Annie looked to the right and left. "There's got to be another way to get to the hospital."

"I think we can go around Cornwall Park and come in from behind." He drove on. The rain came down harder, and he cranked up the wipers.

"Maybe we can cut through the back of that shopping center." Annie pointed to the right at a large grocery store and several small shops.

Alex slowed and scanned the parking lot, but the water looked deeper there than in the street. A pickup truck pulled up behind them and honked. Alex flipped on his emergency flashers and signaled the truck driver to go ahead.

The truck barreled around them into the parking lot, spraying water on both sides like high waves. He seemed to have the same idea of cutting through and disappeared behind the row of stores.

"Maybe we should follow him."

Alex clenched his jaw. It looked risky, but he had to get to the hospital, and there didn't seem to be any other way. He pulled into the parking lot and drove around behind the stores. Dumpsters and piles of wooden crates stood by the back entrances. A few lights shone down on the rear parking lot, illuminating their way.

"The water looks deeper here." Annie's voice rose to a higher pitch. "Maybe we should go back."

He took a quick glance over his shoulder. "We're more

than halfway. We've got to keep going." He gripped the steering wheel and leaned forward.

Only two seconds later, the engine sputtered and died.

Alex twisted the key in the ignition, pumping and giving it more gas, but the engine wouldn't start.

Annie gasped. "We're moving."

Panic shot through Alex as he felt the car lift and turn.

"Mommy," Emma whimpered from the backseat.

Annie grasped his arm. The car tilted and bobbed across the parking lot, picking up speed as it flowed down the slope. The beam of the headlights glowed across the surface of the water and showed they were headed toward a stream.

Alex ripped off his seat belt. "We've got to get out, now."

Annie reached for her door handle.

"No!" Alex lunged and grabbed her. "Not the door. We have to go out the window."

The car spun like a crazy carnival ride. Emma's whimpering cries turned to panicked screams. He stabbed the button to lower the windows, but nothing happened. Energy pumped through him. He had to get them out of this car.

God, please help me. No sooner had he thought the prayer than he had the answer. "Get Emma up here."

Annie unfastened her seat belt and pulled Emma into the front with them.

Alex pushed his seat back as far as possible and tore off his coat. "Turn away. Cover your face and Emma's." Placing his coat over the side window, he leaned back and kicked the glass. A painful jolt fired up his leg, but the window didn't break. *Please, God.* Gritting his teeth, he kicked again. The glass shattered and crumbled around him.

Covering his hand with his coat, he knocked out most of the remaining glass and left his coat lying over the jagged edge. "You need to go first."

Annie stared at him, her eyes wide. "What?"

"Climb up on the roof. I'll hand Emma to you." When she didn't move, he grabbed her arm. "You have to go now."

While Emma's cries grew louder, Annie climbed over Emma and him, then out the window. He held on and boosted her up to the roof.

He turned to Emma. "Your turn, sweetie."

"No!" Emma screamed and clung to him, but he pried her fingers loose and shoved her out the window into Annie's arms. All the while the car bobbed and swayed. Water splashed around his feet and ankles as it started filling the car.

He stood on the seat and hoisted himself out the window. Emma's cries and Annie's frantic efforts to try to calm her daughter cut through the night, sending a frightening chill through him.

His mind spun as he tried to pull his thoughts into focus. A terrifying panic rose in his chest and cut off the air in his throat. This couldn't be happening. Not again.

He could not lose everyone he loved in a wild and rushing flood.

The water pulled the car down the slope and into the stream, spinning it like a wild top. Trees closed in overhead, darkening his view for a few seconds. Moonlight cut through the clouds. The car headed for the bank and crashed into a clump of trees.

Emma screamed, slid off the roof and splashed into the dark, murky water. Without even looking his way, Annie jumped into the swirling flood.

His heart froze. All the air was sucked from his lungs as he watched them disappear into the darkness.

Annie plunged into the water. The icy shock stunned her. Water closed over her head, pulling her under into the churning flood. Kicking and waving her arms like a madwoman, she searched for Emma.

Her daughter screamed off to the left. Annie dived toward the sound, banging into something hard. Pain stabbed her arm. She rose above the surface, straining in the faint moonlight to catch a glimpse of Emma. A swirling wave slapped her face, and she swallowed a gulp of muddy-tasting water. *Please, God, help me find her.*

Emma's head popped up. She gasped and disappeared beneath the icy stream.

Annie pulled in a deep breath and dived again, flailing in her maddening search.

Something soft brushed past her hand. She groped toward it, grasped fabric and hair, and rose to the surface. "Emma!"

Her daughter gasped and lunged toward her, pulling them both down. Alarm raced through Annie. She wrapped her arms tightly around Emma, trying to calm her daughter while she kicked to keep them above water. "I've got you. Lean against me."

Annie could see trees and bushes lining the bank. She kicked in that direction, dragging Emma with her. In a few seconds her feet touched bottom. Emma coughed and cried as she clung to Annie.

With her clothes streaming and feeling like one-hundred-pound weights, Annie climbed out of the water. "It's all right. It's all right."

Holding Emma close, she clawed her way to the top of the bank and sank down in the mud, panting. Water rushed around her, pouring into the stream. She had to get to higher ground before they were pulled in again.

"Where's Alex?" Emma cried in broken sobs.

Annie's mind raced, while terrible dread rose and filled her chest. She pulled herself up and squinted into the darkness toward the raging stream. She shouted his name, but the only sound she heard was the rushing water storming past.

Emma stood and grabbed her hand, her pitiful sobs growing louder.

Annie lifted Emma into her arms, holding her tight as her own tears overflowed. *Oh, God, please.* Her mind felt so numb, it was all she could pray.

Her senses reeled as she tried to pull her thoughts together. One thing was clear. She had to get help. Turning away from the stream, she searched the darkness and spotted the lights of the shopping center in the distance.

Holding her daughter close, she sloshed through the water, each step a painful journey. She'd only gone a few feet when she heard a loud sloshing behind her.

She turned, and her heart jumped in her chest.

Alex trudged up the bank, coughing and panting. "Annie!"

She ran toward him, tears streaming down her face again. He grabbed her and held her and Emma tight. She couldn't speak, but they didn't need words.

Finally he stepped back, but he still held on to her upper arms. "Are you okay?"

She nodded, her tearful smile breaking through at last. "We are now."

Dripping wet, muddy and exhausted from their battle against the flood, they wrapped their arms around each other and walked toward the distant lights.

Chapter Twenty

Alex pulled the blue shirt over his head. One of the E.R. doctors had taken pity on him and found an old pair of scrubs for him to wear, since his clothes were wet and mud-caked. The pants were a little short, but anything was better than that drafty hospital gown.

He tugged the shirt into place while he listened to the nurses coming and going on the other side of the curtain, where they were assessing Annie and Emma.

His nurse, Melissa, pushed the curtain aside, entered his room and handed Alex his discharge forms. "You're all set."

"Thanks." He grabbed the plastic bag filled with his wet clothes. "Any news on my grandmother?"

"I'm sorry. It's been such a crazy night, I forgot to check with the admitting nurse. I'll go do that now."

"Thanks. Are they done next door?"

"Let me see." Melissa slipped past the curtain into Annie and Emma's room. A few seconds later she looked out and smiled. "She says you can come in."

Alex nodded his thanks and entered Annie's room.

Annie lay on the bed with Emma snuggled up beside her. Her daughter slept peacefully with her arm draped over her mother. Annie smiled at him, love and affection filling her eyes.

But he didn't deserve it. His throat tightened as regret and gratitude continued their battle in his mind.

She reached for him and captured his hand in hers. He held on tight for a few seconds before he could speak. "I'm sorry, Annie, so sorry."

She blinked, looking confused. "You mean about the car?"

"About everything." He pulled in a deep breath, struggling to keep his emotions in check. "Going off to Chicago without working things out with you was stupid. I don't know what I was thinking."

"But I didn't really give you a chance to work it out." She clasped his hand more tightly. "I should've been willing to listen to you instead of jumping to conclusions."

"I won't let anything like that separate us again. You mean more to me than any job, no matter what they're offering."

"Thanks, Alex. That means a lot."

"By the time I got to Chicago, I realized my mistake. But tonight when we got pulled into that stream and the water was rising, and I thought I might lose you—" His voice choked off and he looked down. "You mean so much to me. I can't believe I…" But he couldn't finish his sentence. The weight on his heart was too heavy.

"What is it, Alex?"

He straightened and looked down at her. "When Emma fell in, you didn't hesitate. You jumped right in after her."

"Of course. She's my daughter."

He held her gaze for a second. "But I didn't. I froze."

Her eyes widened, then filled with sympathy. "Oh, Alex—"

He lifted his hand. "Please. I want to get this out. It's not an excuse, but when I saw Emma fall in the water and you jump in after her, I felt like I was twelve again, caught in the flood, watching my dad try to save me."

"That must've been terrible."

"It was like I was in a wrestling match against my fear. It took me a few seconds before I could get past that and jump in."

"But you did." She smiled, assurance in her eyes.

He shook his head, still feeling like a coward, knowing she was the one who had to save Emma. "You could've both drowned, and it would've been my fault."

"No, that's not true. Listen to me. When the engine died and we were trapped in the car, I was so scared I couldn't think straight. But you stayed calm and thought of a way to get us out. I don't know if I would've thought to kick out the window, and even if I'd thought of the idea, I don't know if I would've had the strength to do it." She wrapped both her hands around his. "This is the truth. Emma and I would've died in that car tonight without you. Your strength and quick thinking are what saved our lives."

He let her words wash over his heart, soothing the sting of self-doubt and condemnation. He still wished he would've acted more quickly, but in the end he'd beat out his fears, jumped in the water and searched for Annie and Emma until he found them. That was enough for Annie, and he had to let that be enough for him.

He reached for her and hugged her tightly. "I love you, Annie."

"I love you, too, so very much." She kissed his cheek, then leaned back until she could look him in the eyes. "Please, Alex, let's give God the credit for saving us all tonight and be thankful."

His chest expanded, and he nodded. Then he leaned down and kissed her, more grateful than ever for her gracious love and forgiving heart.

The curtain swished back. "Alex? Annie?"

Alex turned, and his eyes widened.

His grandmother stood there, dressed and smiling, with her Bayside Treasure friends clustered around her. "Well, for goodness' sake, it is you. The nurse told me you were here. What happened?"

"We had an accident on the way to the hospital, but we're okay. How are you?"

"I'm fine. They ran all kinds of tests. The doctor says it was probably just heartburn from overeating." Her face flushed, and she held up her hand. "I know, Annie warned me not to overdo it. But I promise I've learned my lesson this time."

Alex shook his head as he grinned at his grandmother. "I certainly hope so."

Marian tugged on Irene's arm. "I think we should go and let them finish...you know."

Irene's eyes lit up. "Good idea. We'll just step out so you two can have a little privacy."

"We're sorry we interrupted you," Barb added. "Just go back to whatever you were doing."

Hannah's eyes twinkled. "I told them there was nothing to worry about. Sooner or later you two were going to realize you were perfect for each other."

"Now, girls, we don't want to be sticking our noses in their business," Irene added.

"Oh, no, we'd never do that." Hannah snickered and grabbed Marian's arm. "We just pray and see what the Lord has in mind when it comes to matters of the heart."

"That's right," Irene said with a decisive nod. "We pray and wait for Him to move."

Barb chuckled. "Well, sometimes we do like to help Him along...just a little."

"Come on, girls." His grandmother herded her friends out

to the hallway. Then she turned, winked at Alex and pulled the curtain closed behind her.

Annie laughed softly and shook her head. "They are so cute."

Alex nodded, then leaned in closer. "Now, where were we?"

"I think we were right here." With her eyes sparkling, she smiled and tapped her lips.

"Oh, yes, now I remember." He bent closer, her eyes slid closed and he kissed her like a thirsty man who'd found a sweet mountain stream.

Epilogue

Annie wrapped her red scarf more tightly around her neck and scanned the bustling crowd gathered on the sidewalk in front of the newly remodeled Jameson's Bakery Café. The sign announcing the grand reopening fluttered in a cool breeze drifting in from Bellingham Bay. The ribbon-cutting ceremony was due to start in five minutes.

Emma grasped her mother's hand. "There sure are a lot of people here."

"Yes, there are." Annie's heart warmed, thankful that so many had come out to share this special time with them.

Irene stood near the front door with her Bayside Treasure friends clustered around her. The women were all dressed in warm coats and hats to protect themselves from the chilly weather as they chatted and greeted friends and neighbors.

Annie scanned the sea of faces, looking for Alex. She spotted him standing on the far side of the crowd with Ross and Adrie Peterson. Ross managed a nearby photography studio and had recently married Adrie, who was Marian Chandler's granddaughter. Adrie and Ross had met at Bayside Books almost a year ago when he took over as manager so she could pursue a music career. But she fell in love with Ross and decided to stay in Fairhaven instead. Now Adrie gave music lessons to foster children and played her flute in the Whatcom Symphony.

Ross and Adrie made a lovely couple. Annie couldn't be happier for them. She smiled, remembering how Irene and the Bayside Treasures had helped bring them together through their matchmaking plans and prayers. They seemed to have quite a talent for matching up their younger friends and relatives, including her and Alex.

She called Alex's name and waved to him.

He caught sight of her and returned her smile and wave. After a few more words to Ross and Adrie, he made his way through the crowd toward her. "I was wondering where you were." He leaned down and kissed her cheek.

"Emma's gymnastics class ran late."

Alex laid his hand on Emma's shoulder. "How'd it go?"

She looked up and sent him a proud smile. "I walked on the balance beam."

"Good for you. I knew you could do it." He gave her a hug, then stood and pulled his phone from his coat pocket. "It's time to get started."

Annie nodded and gazed up at the bakery with its beautiful old brick exterior, freshly painted trim, new sign and awnings. Small evergreens filled the planters by the front door, and Annie could imagine how nice they'd look in the spring, filled with tulips. Maybe she'd plant geraniums in the summer.

"Hi, Annie. Alex." Jason approached with his daughter, Faith, and a few of the men who'd worked with him on the remodeling project. Faith and Emma exchanged smiles.

"The bakery looks great, inside and out." Alex held out his hand to Jason. "You did a terrific job."

"Thanks. I have a good crew."

"We're grateful," Alex added. "It's not often you hear about a renovation job finishing on time and under budget."

Jason chuckled. "That's true." He shifted his gaze to Annie. "But I said I'd give you my best."

"And you have," Annie said with a smile. "Thank you."

A more comfortable friendship had developed between all of them in the past month after Alex announced he'd be staying in Fairhaven and managing the bakery with Annie. Jason and Faith had come over for dessert on New Year's Eve, and Annie had watched Faith a few times for Jason.

Irene called to Annie and Alex and motioned for them to join her by the front door.

"I'll let you go," Jason said, stepping back.

Emma tugged on Annie's hand. "Can I watch with Faith?"

Annie glanced at Jason.

"I'll keep an eye on her," he said.

Annie leaned down to Emma's eye level. "Okay. Be sure to stay with Faith and Jason."

"I will." Emma clasped Faith's hand and followed Jason a few feet away to where they'd have a good view for the ribbon cutting.

Alex slipped his hand into Annie's. "Time to get this party started." Warmth and confidence flowed through his fingers into hers.

Delightful tingles traveled up her arm. Sharing this day with Alex and Irene meant so much to her she could barely contain her happiness.

They joined Irene and stood in front of the entrance.

Walter Morris, the president of the Old Fairhaven Association, held up his hand. "Can I have your attention, please?" The crowd quieted. "We're here today to celebrate the reopening of one of Fairhaven's finest businesses, Jameson's Bakery, now known as Jameson's Bakery Café. We want to offer our hearty congratulations and best wishes to the owner, Irene Jameson, and to the new managers, Alex Jameson and Annie Romano. We hope you'll enjoy many more years of successful business in our community." The crowd clapped. "And now Pastor James from Grace Chapel will say a prayer of blessing."

The pastor stepped forward, and the crowd hushed and bowed their heads. "Father, thank You for the way You've blessed Irene over the years and allowed her to operate her business and provide such delicious food to our community. We ask now that You'll continue to oversee the operation of Jameson's Bakery Café. Bless all who work here and all who enter these doors. In Jesus's Name, Amen."

The crowd clapped again.

Marian Chandler unrolled a bright red spool of ribbon and passed one end to Hannah Bodine. They stretched it across the doorway and looked expectantly at Irene.

She took the scissors from her purse and held them out to Alex.

"No, Gram," he whispered. "You should cut the ribbon."

She placed the scissors in his hand. "I want you and Annie to do it together."

Alex's eyes softened, and he kissed his grandmother's cheek then shifted his gaze to Annie.

She stepped forward and laid her hand over his, and together they cut the ribbon. The crowd cheered, and soon everyone was shaking their hands or patting them on the back.

"Come on inside," Irene called. "We've got hot coffee and bakery treats for everyone!"

Annie and Alex stood back, greeting people as they walked toward the front door. Soon most of the crowd had moved inside.

"Hey, look, it's snowing!" Emma danced around, holding hands with Faith. The girls laughed and tipped their faces up to catch the puffy flakes on their cheeks.

Annie gave them another minute, then called Emma. "Come on inside, sweetie."

Jason herded the girls toward the entrance. Annie was about to follow them inside, but Alex caught her hand.

"Wait a minute." He smiled, and a mischievous twinkle lit up his eyes.

Her heart fluttered. "How come?"

"I was hoping for a minute alone with you."

She sent him a teasing smile. "I don't know. It's awfully cold out here."

He slipped his arms around her, pulling her close. "Don't worry. I'll keep you warm."

She snuggled against him, savoring the comfort and safety of his arms. This was the love she had waited so long to find. And God was the one who'd guided her home and brought them together. Thankfulness rose from her heart in a silent prayer, and she sensed His blessing on their future together.

Emma leaned out the door. "Hey, are you coming? Gram's gonna cut the cake."

"Be right there," Annie called over her shoulder. She turned back to Alex and smiled up at him, drinking in the look of love that shone in his eyes.

"Cake sounds good," he said, "but I have something sweeter in mind."

"And what might that be?" she asked, her heart overflowing with happiness.

"A kiss from my sweetheart." He leaned down, his breath a warm whisper against her cheek.

She lifted her lips to meet his. Then she kissed him sweetly and tenderly while lacy snowflakes fluttered around them in a swirling dance.

* * * * *

If you enjoyed Carrie Turansky's book, be sure to check out the other books this month from Love Inspired!

Dear Reader,

Thanks so much for joining me on this third journey to Fairhaven. I hope you enjoyed getting to know Alex, Annie, Emma, Irene and her Bayside Treasure friends. Their story highlights the importance of allowing God to heal hurts we have carried with us from the past so we can enjoy healthy and meaningful relationships in the present. We may not understand the pain or losses we've experienced in our lives, but we can hold on to God and trust His love for us. He offers that love and forgiveness to everyone who comes to Him. He waits for you with open arms.

If you missed the first two stories set in Fairhaven, I hope you will look for them online. *Seeking His Love* tells Cam and Rachel's story. *A Man to Trust* tells Ross and Adrie's story. And the Bayside Treasure ladies appear in each book.

I would love to connect with you via email, Facebook, Pinterest or Twitter. I offer an email newsletter every other month with book news, encouraging articles, reading recommendations, recipes, photos and more. You can contact me and sign up for the newsletter at my website: www.carrieturansky.com.

Carrie Turansky

Questions for Discussion

1. Annie's memories of being alone in the hospital prompted her to feel compassion for Irene when she had her heart attack. Have you ever gone through a difficult experience like that? Has it given you compassion for others going through a similar circumstance?

2. Alex loved his grandmother, but he allowed work and other interests to take priority over visits home. But when his grandmother had a heart attack, he realized how important she was to him. Do you make an effort to spend time with family members and let them know how special they are to you?

3. Irene had to make changes in her lifestyle and eating habits after her heart attack, and it was challenging for her. Have you ever had to make changes like that? What helped you the most in coping with those changes?

4. Emma realized she was different because she didn't have a relationship with her father like her friends did. What were some of the ways she coped with that issue? How would you help a child like Emma?

5. Being a single parent wasn't easy for Annie. What were some of the struggles she faced because she was raising Emma on her own? How could you reach out and help a single parent?

6. Alex focused on his career rather than building relationships with God and people. Because of his past, he

realized there was a risk of losing someone he loved, so he held back. Do you step out and take risks in relationships? Why or why not?

7. Alex found strength and direction as he began praying and taking his struggles to God. Do you talk to God about the struggles in your life? Have you experienced the peace God provides through prayer?

8. Annie loved to cook for friends and family. She used her gifts and talents to bless and help others. What gifts or talents do you have that you could use to bless someone else?

9. When Alex, Annie and Emma were caught in the flood, Alex wrestled against his fear and overcame it to help Annie and Emma. Have you ever faced a fearful situation and overcome your fear?

10. Irene has a special connection with her Bayside Treasure friends. The love and care they showed her was an important part of her recovery. Do you have friends who are a support to you? What could you do to strengthen those friendships?

11. Emma adds a lot of fun to this story. What was your favorite scene including Emma?

12. Annie realized forgiveness is not a onetime event but an ongoing process. She learned to take her hurt and painful memories to the Lord each time they came to mind,

and forgive again. Is there someone you've struggled to forgive? Could you take that to the Lord and ask Him to help you peel away the next layer?

COMING NEXT MONTH from Love Inspired®
AVAILABLE DECEMBER 18, 2012

RANCHER'S REFUGE
Whisper Falls
Linda Goodnight
Both running from their pasts, Annalisa Keller and Austin Blackwell learn that painful secrets are washed away beneath Whisper Falls—where prayers actually are answered.

HOMECOMING REUNION
Home to Hartley Creek
Carolyne Aarsen
Garret Beck always thought money gave him control over life, but reconnecting with first love Larissa Weir makes him question what really matters.

FALLING FOR THE FOREST RANGER
Leigh Bale
The dangers of the untamed Idaho rivers drive Tanner Bohlman to protect Zoë Lawton and her son, even if the beautiful marine biologist has more grit than he gives her credit for!

DOCTOR TO THE RESCUE
Eagle Point Emergency
Cheryl Wyatt
When she agrees to babysit former combat doctor Ian Shupe's little girl, Bri Landis has her heart touched by father *and* daughter as both struggle to trust again.

SMALL-TOWN DAD
Jean C. Gordon
Wanting to recapture the life he lost while raising his daughter alone, Neil Hazard can't possibly let Anne Howard and her precious toddler into his future—can he?

A DAUGHTER'S REDEMPTION
Georgiana Daniels
Robyn Warner has unknowingly fallen for the cop responsible for her father's death...but Caleb Sloane just can't bring himself to walk away from the grieving woman.

LICNM1212

REQUEST YOUR FREE BOOKS!

2 FREE INSPIRATIONAL NOVELS
PLUS 2
FREE
MYSTERY GIFTS

*Brave police officers tackle crime with the help of their
canine partners in* TEXAS K-9 UNIT, *an exciting
new series from Love Inspired® Suspense.*

Read on for a preview of the first book,
TRACKING JUSTICE by Shirlee McCoy.

Police detective Austin Black glanced at his dashboard
clock as he raced up Oak Drive. Two in the morning. Not a
good time to get a call about a missing child.

Then again, there was never a good time for that; never
a good time to look in the worried eyes of a parent or to
follow a scent trail and know that it might lead to a joyful
reunion or a sorrowful goodbye.

If it led anywhere.

Sometimes trails went cold, scents were lost and the
missing were never found. Austin wanted to bring them all
home safe. Hopefully, this time, he would.

He pulled into the driveway of a small house.

Justice whined. A three-year-old bloodhound, he was
trained in search and rescue and knew when it was time
to work.

Austin jumped out of the vehicle when a woman darted
out the front door. "You called about a missing child?"

"Yes. My son. I heard Brady call for me, and when I
walked into his room, he was gone." She ran back up the
porch stairs.

Austin jogged in after her. She waved from a doorway.
"This is my son's room."

Austin followed her into the room. "How old is your son, Ms….?"

"Billows. Eva. He's seven."

"Did you argue?"

"We didn't argue about anything, Officer…"

"Detective Austin Black. I'm with Sagebrush Police Department's Special Operation K-9 Unit."

"You have a search dog with you?" Her face brightened. "I can give you something of his. A shirt or—"

"Hold on. I need to get a little more information first."

"How about you start out there?" She gestured to the window.

"Was it open when you came in the room?"

"Yes. It looks like someone carried Brady out the window. But I don't know how anyone could have gotten into his room when all the doors and windows were locked."

"You're sure?"

"Of course." She frowned. "I always double-check. I have ever since…"

"What?"

"Nothing that matters. I just need to find my son."

Hiding something?

"Everything matters when a child is missing, Eva."

To see Justice the bloodhound in action, pick up
TRACKING JUSTICE by Shirlee McCoy.
Available January 2013 from Love Inspired® Suspense.

Linda Goodnight

brings you a tale of a cowboy you can trust.

Rancher Austin Blackwell sees Annalisa Keller as a wounded
person with too many secrets. This town is the perfect
place for her to start over—just as it was for him. Trying to
keep his own past hidden, Austin finds himself falling for
Annalisa, whose warmth and love of life works its way
into his heart…and promises never to leave.

Rancher's Refuge

Where every prayer is answered….

Available December 2012, wherever books are sold.

www.LoveInspiredBooks.com

LI87787